TILL DEATH

TILL DEATH

Jennifer M Edmisten

This is a work of fiction. Names, characters, places and incidents either are the
product of the author's imagination or are used fictitiously, and any resemblance
to any actual persons, living or dead, events, or locales is entirely coincidental.

Any people depicted in stock imagery provided by Thinkstock are models,
and such images are being used for illustrative purposes only.
Certain stock imagery © Thinkstock.

Print information available on the last page.

Rev. date: 06/17/2016

To order additional copies of this book, contact:
Xlibris
1-888-795-4274
www.Xlibris.com
Orders@Xlibris.com
741652

Bishop Malwin didn't give any visual acknowledgment to the guard but instead took a stance in front of the locked cell door to observe its occupant. He could hear hushed whispers emanate from the sullen figure in the corner. What was being said was only recognized by the bishop and one other accompanying him. The piercing coal-black stare of the lavishly clothed man didn't blink in their continuous deciphering of the enigmatic language.

Standing quietly to the bishop's left was a priest, a silver cross necklace standing out in contrast to his black robes. His intense gray eyes squared down on the detained. "The blood is born, again . . . two hundred and fifty years later."

The bishop parted his pursed lips to question the detained. "Where is the blood being born? Where might we find the child?"

A strained, hoarse moan was the only answer the woman had to give. Quietly, Bishop Malwin turned his head to gaze at the jittery form of Jamos. "Open the cell."

Without questioning the order, the guard did as told and rejoined Barten along the back wall. Bishop Malwin then brought his gaze over to the leftward priest. A nod of his head gave a silent order, and the priest glided past and into the dungeon cell.

He towered over the wretched woman to interrogate. "The babe is close, isn't it? You can sense it. Tell me where, Lady Ryna."

Bloodshot eyes shifted in their sockets to meet the priest's chilling stare. "He knows and is searching. They all know, but he . . . *he* is whom you should dread."

The name "Caliss" rolled off the priest's tongue in a growl.

A glint of anger shined in the priest's eyes for only a moment, bringing a sinister smile from the Lady Ryna.

Bishop Malwin's nostrils flared and his jaw muscles flexed in anger. "Abbot Christophe," he began in a booming voice, "assemble a team of our finest and comb the nearby lands for the child." He and Lady Ryna's eyes locked on each other's. The man continued in a stern tone. "We must not let one of the last of Lilith's chosen obtain the blood."

The priest Abbot Christophe left the cell and ordered over his shoulder in passing, "Brother Henry, you will be accompanying me."

The monk, who had been standing quietly, did as told and joined the abbot's pace.

As per order of the Sect, a team of horses and all monks trained in specialized combat were always on standby. One never knew when word would come from the bishop to mount up for a defensive or offensive measure against the damned. It was because of this that the selected team, led by Abbot Christophe, was ready for departure. Four monks were on horseback while another steered a small carriage the abbot rode in. Also inside the carriage was Brother Henry.

His hands were busy securing the curtains of the carriage's interior shut while Abbot Christophe watched him. "Remember your training, boy." Brother Henry stopped in his working to meet the firm stare of his mentor. "Do whatever is necessary to protect the child should we find them alive and unharmed."

The timid monk hesitantly nodded his head to oblige. "Yes, Abbot."

2

It Has Begun

Every house of every known village was searched in the immediate area. But just as Lady Ryna had stated, they weren't the only ones on the hunt. During the priest and monks' searching, they came across a settlement roughly two days' ride from their starting point.

The sight was horrific in the failing evening sunlight. Blood painted the muddy streets and pooled where mutilated bodies lay. One of the monks brought his horse to a stop and was mindful where he dismounted. The carriage door opened to reveal Abbot Christophe looking grief stricken and sorrowful.

Before even witnessing the sight himself, he had an expectation of what he was about to see. There was no mistaking the putrid stench of flesh starting to rot filling the air. His footsteps sloshed about the mud in his striding through the streets to personally investigate the carnage. Behind him was Brother Henry, holding a sleeved hand to his face.

He forced back a gag to question, "What happened here? Was it . . . *them?*" Abbot Christophe nodded.

Another monk, head shaven bald and brown eyes scanning the many bodies, deeply exhaled a quiet sob. "These people didn't deserve this." He jerked his head around to look at the priest. "Was this the work of Caliss?"

"No, Brother Andrew," came the abbot's response. "This is just the act of a stray, starving pack having no coven."

"Do you think they are still near?" The monk's eyes returned to searching the many structures of the settlement.

The priest was silent and held up a hand for others to hush themselves as well. All fell quiet when listening to the eerie calm around them. There were no crickets chirping to sing in the night. No wind blowing. Nothing. But Abbot Christophe's head snapping toward a hut not far from where he stood brought forth curiosity from those around him.

He was thoughtful of his steps in proximity to the deceased, but he cared not for the blood on the streets staining his shoes and robes. The monks watched him near the hut and approach the door with no regard for caution. His fingertips pushed open the already-cracked door to reveal a gruesome sight within.

Scattered on the floor were slashed and dismembered bodies. Huddled in a corner was a young woman wearing clothing drenched in blood. She bad been badly injured as she held a crimson rag to a gash at her neck. Almost all color was drained from her as was much of her blood. Abbot Christophe had seen situations like this many times in the past and felt pained for the woman's fate.

Her gaze weakly fell on him and strained to focus on the black-robed man. The priest knelt down to gently pry the rag away from the swollen, torn flesh on her neck and frowned. He then brought a hand to her mouth and upturned her upper lip to reveal her partially elongating canines. She was in the early stages of an adverse transformation and nodded in understanding of the dire situation.

He calmly spoke. "Do you remember what happened?"

A labored "Y-yes" came from the woman's chapped lips.

"Demons of the night . . . beasts of blood . . . they did this, didn't they?" Subtle nodding came from the waning woman. "Were there any newborns to this settlement from two nights past?"

The woman barely whispered her answer. "No."

Abbot Christophe nodded and gently rested a hand on the woman's forehead. For someone near death, her body was burning up with fever. This, too, signified her body's transformation. "Do you know what will become of you, shortly?" She shook her head. "You will become of that which attacked you. A damned life of pain and eternal agony, unless . . . you let me help you." Her face wrinkled up in hopeless sadness. "You know what I must do."

Though there was no voice, the woman's words could still be made out. "I don't want to be like them."

"Very well." With that, the man removed his silver cross necklace from around his neck and extracted a concealed blade within it. "Forgive me, my child."

A scheming smile deepened the wrinkles in the abbess's features. "Knowing you, you have already done what was needed to cleanse those places of evil. As far as your requesting assistance, I know just the person. You might remember her." Mary slimmed her eyes beneath an arched brow. "Sister Frances?"

Christophe's expression mirrored the woman's. "Do I. She was only the best in her training section by a broad margin. Of course, that was only twenty-something years ago."

"Only a blink of an eye for you, I'm sure," Mary stated with a smirk. "Well, I can assure you, her skills have greatly improved since then. You won't be disappointed."

"I wasn't disappointed then, when she was barely sixteen. I more than trust your judgment, Abbess Mary. She will also be needed to personally care for the child hereafter."

Quiet debate filled the elder woman's eyes. "Very well. I will relay the message to her after our morning service. You and your brothers will be joining us, won't you? It would be an honor to have you lead us in prayer."

The abbot couldn't have been more touched by the request. "Of course, Abbess."

*　　*　　*　　*

Once the last of the supplies needed for the trip back to the Vatican were secured to the carriage, the accompanying monks mounted their horses.

Abbot Christophe and Brother Henry patiently waited by the carriage for Sister Frances to arrive with the baby. The concern Henry harbored within him was intensifying the brighter the dusk-filled sky became. He could see where the early-morning sun was soon to peek over the horizon to the right of the abbey. His worry-stricken green eyes kept shifting between the rising sun and Christophe. Why wasn't the abbot equally worried, if not more? If he was, he was concealing it amazingly well.

Still, the abbot's gray eyes stayed focused on the wide-open double wooden doors of the abbey. He could hear the voices of discussing women become louder the closer they got to the door. Abbess Mary was the first to emerge, followed by Sister Frances and two other joining nuns.

A smile stretched across Christophe's features. Those same brilliant blue eyes of the nun were still the same as he remembered from years past.

Mary patted the sister on the back in comfort and gestured her to load onto the carriage. "Best you be on your way and may God bless your path."

Sister Frances went into the carriage, followed by Brother Henry. Christophe warmly smiled at the abbess. "Do not worry for the child, for she will be in good hands from this day forward."

"You are one of the very few I trust the blood with, Abbot. Do not let me down."

"Wouldn't dream of it." He lightly chuckled. "Farewell, Abbess Mary." Just moments after he stepped into the carriage and the door was secured shut, the first morning sunrays shone upon the land.

The lazy blue eyes of Daniela, still learning how to focus on the new world around them, stared upward at Sister Frances. Her little hand wiggled through the blankets she was wrapped in and grabbed onto the first thing she could. Tiny fingers held tightly to the shiny silver cross around the nun's neck.

Sister Frances smiled and held the baby's hand in her own. "One day, little one, this will be yours to protect you from the evils of this world." She kissed the little hand and repeated, "One day, little Daniela . . ."

5

Rendezvous

The day was panning out to be a nice, relaxing ride. Overhead clouds provided some protection from the sun, which William was grateful for. With the risen sun came warmer temperatures. Temperatures both monks knew to enjoy when they could. Once the sun started to set, the unpleasant chill would return.

Midafternoon the monks stopped on the side of the road to rest the horse. Meanwhile, they split a loaf of bread and some cheese between them for lunch. Off in the distance loomed a thundercloud.

Julian sternly warned, "So help me, Will, if you say it I'll leave you here by yourself."

William looked to his travel companion. "Say what? I wasn't going to say anything." The older man tore a chunk out of his bread and slowly chewed it. "Unless, of course, you're referring to the storm cloud—"

"I'm warning you. Don't say it." He swallowed down his bite with a hefty drink of water. "As long as your mouth stays closed, that storm stays over there."

William rolled his eyes and finished his lunch. "Just so you know, it's your turn to drive the carriage." He reached over to a rolled-up piece of parchment on the ground next to him and unrolled it. It was a map and their path traced over with heavy ink. "We should be right about here. This town here"—he pointed to a small drawing of buildings—"is just over that hill, there." The monk gestured to a hill's rise a little ways down the road. "That is our halfway point. Our next stop is a little over half a day's ride to here." William's finger lingered over a larger drawn collection of buildings. "From there, we swap out the horse and ride on to the nunnery to pick up her ladyship."

Julian shoved a bite of cheese into his mouth and nodded in understanding. "Got it." After the last bites of cheese and bread were finished up, he stood up and dusted the crumbs off the front of his robe. "I'm glad you plotted a course. Makes traveling a lot easier."

William scoffed and stuffed the extra food back into his travel bag. "Someone has to be responsible."

The two men resumed their journey, Julian carefully watching the storm pass over the landscape before them. Farther on down the path, the solid dirt of the road had become mud. The rain from the passing storm had drenched the lands.

The older monk sneered to the younger. "See? This is what happens when you don't say that damned line." A harsh elbow to his ribs made him flinch and rub his side. "What was that for?"

"Watch your mouth, *Brother*. I do not condone profanity and you shouldn't either." William glared at the carriage driver, who was snickering to himself.

*   *   *   *

Their route later took them along a narrow path walled by trees on one side and a steep drop off on the other. Should two carriages encounter each other on the road, it would require careful negotiation of both drivers to avoid sending one or the other off the ledge.

Today was a different kind of negotiation. A section of the road had been washed out, and trying to cross over it would potentially mean damage to the wagon. Turning around would be just as tricky, if even possible at all.

William grumbled in annoyance and studied the immediate area. "The trees are too close together to try weaving around them and I'm not even chancing down there." Both monks leaned over to look down the slope.

Julian got out of the front seat and stood over the washout. Jagged rocks could be seen poking out from beneath the mud. "The deepest part is only knee-deep. Let's unload the sacks from the wagon and try crossing it. The less weight the better."

William frowned in skepticism. "Must we? Some of those sacks are quite heavy."

"If we try crossing this with the wagon loaded down, the weight will cause the wheels to sink into the mud. I don't know about you, but I'd rather not get stuck." Julian studied the other monk and sat his hands on his hips, awaiting an answer. "So what's it going to be?"

Meanwhile, inside the abbey's chapel, begging whispers of a young woman turned into desperate pleas as tears streamed from green eyes. They stared up to a wooden cross hanging on the far wall of the candlelit chapel. "Please, my heavenly Father, blessed be my path in the journey that lies ahead. My heart is with you, Lord. Please, protect me. Do not let me die to those demons!"

Heavy doors leading to the chapel startled the young woman. A slightly older woman rushed down the red carpet aisle in frantic breaths, announcing, "My Lady Daniela, come! The brothers are here!" The novitiate nun grabbed the young woman's arm and pulled her to her feet, tugging her to follow.

The young woman stammered, "Sister Elaine, I—" But her sentence was cut off by the other woman.

"Quickly, child, we haven't much time!" The two women left the chapel and entered a hallway lit by lanterns hanging from the walls. "That way when the sun does rise, you will have a head start and can get farther in your travels under its protection. You have a long journey ahead of you, love."

Another nun briskly walking down the hallway neared them, calling out, "Hurry, ladies!"

Daniela reached for the black velvet cloak the approaching nun handed her and draped it over her shoulders. "Thank you, Sister Ella. My bags—"

"Are already loaded in the wagon." Sister Ella took hold of Daniela's other arm and matched her pace in stride.

The three rounded a corner and were on approach toward the open wooden door when Daniela froze in her steps. She hoped the sun would have risen by now, but in finding it hadn't, she completely changed her mind. "Oh no, no, no! I'm not going out there! The sun hasn't even completely risen yet!"

Abbess Francis could hear vocal scuffling among the women in the hallway, and apparently, so could the monks preparing the wagon for their return journey. She could sense she was being watched and shifted her gaze between the pairs of eyes peering at her from over the wagon.

She took in a deep breath and spoke in a patient tone of voice. "You must forgive the girl, Brothers, for Miss Daniela does not travel well."

William whimpered, "Oh no." He grimaced at a memory still all too fresh in his mind and ran a hand over the front of his robe in reaction. "I finally got these cleaned after Julian threw up on me after eating Henry's meatloaf two days back!"

Abbess Frances raised an eyebrow in question and responded in a curt voice, "That's not exactly what I meant, Brother William. I was referring to her anxiety of traveling, particularly those of long distances, given her *condition.*"

Daniela called from within the convent once again with a sterner voice. "I will not leave until the sun has completely risen!"

Ella continued to tug on the woman's arm in urgency. "It might as well be! No creature would chance wondering about, especially given how soon the sun is due to rise."

Abbess Frances glanced back over her shoulder to the hallway doors and stated to the two men, "Excuse me, Brothers." She briskly strode down the walkway and to the opened door, disappearing inside. Her piercing eyes sharpened down on Daniela. The much younger woman could feel the intense sting of the scowl and recoiled. "Do I need to drag you out of this abbey myself?"

Daniela fervently shook her head. Abbess Frances gestured to the door, and the girl obeyed, gathering her cloak around her and sulking to the open door. Daniela peered over her shoulder to see the abbess at her heels. Not wanting to chance further reproach, she hurried outside. She didn't get too far outside once she felt the icy winds tear through her clothing.

Elaine was back at the younger woman's side, stating, "What are you waiting on, child?"

With a firm tug, Daniela was moving forward, but even more so unwillingly than before. Her gaze fell on the horizon to see the glow of the sun's radiance highlight the cloud-free skies. Hopefully the skies would remain clear and allow for a sun-filled trip for the journey's duration.

William studied Julian standing beside him and narrowed his eyes in a frown at the awestruck expression smeared across the other's face. "*Brother* Julian, will you be steering the wagon the first half of the trip or the last?"

But Julian was too distracted with the arrival of the young woman named Daniela. Her skin was like the finest of ivory and her emerald eyes enough to make the most precious of gems jealous.

The addressed monk nodded his head, completely oblivious to the question. "Yeah, sure, sounds good."

"You aren't even listening, are you?"

Before the befuddled monk could mindlessly answer, Elaine cut him off as she approached the two. "Brothers, this is Miss Daniela. My lady, meet Brothers William"—he smiled and nodded—"and Julian."

The last monk kept his eyes locked onto the young woman's and lowered his head in a respectful nod. "My lady."

A generous smile crept across the woman's face, and she curtsied. "Brothers."

Her gaze lingered on Julian's far longer than it should have. Suddenly aware of this and fearing another verbal reprimand, Daniela broke her watch off the older of the two monks.

She rounded the carriage to the back and was about to lower the latched tailgate when Julian intercepted, boyishly smiling. "Here, allow me."

He lowered the gate and offered a hand to the woman, which she gladly took and used to steady herself, stating, "Thank you," climbing into the back of the hay-lined wagon bed.

Abbess Frances sighed upon watching the younger man's actions and sternly met the gaze of William, appearing equally annoyed. She spoke in a voice barely above a whisper. "This had better not come to be a problem, later. I've heard plenty from Father Christophe of your brother's past transgressions."

William shook his head, responding, "I'll personally make sure it doesn't, Abbess Frances," and climbed into the back of the carriage as well.

She was skeptical of this, however, and approached the wagon bed to speak to Daniela. "Do not forget what I taught you, child."

The lowering of the abbess's brow brought a slight recoil from the young woman, and she nodded. "Yes, Abbess."

Julian finished latching the back tailgate of the wagon and proceeded to the front bench seat. He was doing his best to avoid meeting the scrutinizing stare he knew he was receiving from the abbess.

A bit uncomfortably, he sat down and took the horse reins in his hand. He spoke and nodded to the small group of nuns nearby, "Sisters . . ." And finally to the beady silver-blue eyes of the abbess. "Abbess Frances." He cracked the reins, and the carriage lurched forward.

7

A Brother's Tale

Daniela coiled up beneath a wool blanket where she had taken to sitting and watched the nunnery disappear behind a hill. This was her first time ever leaving the holy grounds since arriving twenty-five years ago, and she frowned. She hoped the move was for the best. Seated adjacent to her in the wagon bed was William, his eyes heavily resting on the troubled young woman.

Deciding to make conversation, the monk spoke. "Everything will be fine, my lady. You're in safe hands, I assure you."

She tried to force a reassuring smile, if not for the man, then for herself. "The church has kept me in safe hands thus far. Why stop now?" She grumbled against the frigid winds swallowing what warmth she could hold on to from within.

William, too, felt the gust of wind and rewrapped himself within his robe and cloak. He knew he should've packed a spare blanket. "Could be worse, I suppose . . ." His hazel eyes locked onto the curious green ones of the woman. "Could be raining."

Julian chuckled. "Trying to hex us again, like you did last time?"

Daniela's attention remained focused on the monk near her, and she slightly tilted her head to the side, smiling. "Last time? Exactly how many damsels in distress have you two rescued?"

William explained what was being referred to. "We got rained on shortly after leaving the monastery."

Julian continued from his steering the wagon. "Yeah, and right after he basically said the same thing too."

William shook his head and scoffed. The woman was uncomfortable with how awkward the environment shared between the two monks felt and decided to change the subject. "So tell me, Brother William, how old were you when you decided to join the church?"

The addressed man shifted where he sat and sighed the reply, "Eight."

"Respectable age. May I ask why?" Frustrated hazel eyes squared down on Daniela, and she frowned. "My apologies, Brother, I didn't mean to be nosy. It's none of my business anyway."

William bit back what he really wanted to say and decided to take his frustration out on a straw of hay. There was no need to take his aggravations out on the young woman as he knew she was only trying to make harmless conversation. "No, my lady, it's fine." He cleared his throat and continued. "I, uh, joined the church with the desire to better myself as a person." Their eyes met, and he grimaced, knowing there were times he had lost touch with this goal. "I felt insignificant as a child. Nothing much to brag about when growing up hungry because money was in short supply. I watched my parents struggle to do their best to provide for my brother and I, and felt that in some way, by joining the church, I'd be helping them. And besides, nothing can be more noble than a person devoting their life solely to God and serving his purpose." He released a shudder against a wind gust charging over the top of another hill. He drew his knees to his chest in an effort to stay warm.

Daniela felt a bit warmer inside thinking about the man's words. "How did you end up with the Sect, of all places? I mean, the church keeps it and its purpose under extreme secrecy. Surely it's not something openly talked about to altar boys."

Another chuckle escaped Julian as he replied, "Oh, I don't know. I found out from a recruitment poster nailed to a post." Harshly and without hesitation, William reached over and slapped the other man in the back of the head. "Might want to watch out, I do have a weapon in my possession."

"Neither you nor your *stick* scare me, *Brother*." Daniela ignored Julian's sarcasm and kept her attention focused on William. He gave a final disapproving gawk to the older man seated in the front of the carriage before returning his watch back to the young woman. "And to answer your question, Miss Daniela, I was approached with an offer to do more for God. Everyone knew I wasn't completely satisfied with what I was being spoon-fed to believe when told I was doing everything I could. I knew there had to be more I could do and when I was fourteen, was transferred to Abbot Christophe's monastery. I was told I'd be fighting the spawns of Satan, if not the devil himself, by agreeing to the transfer. I was in London before that. Now here I am."

"Do you regret it? Your decision, that is . . ."

A warm smile brightened the otherwise cold features of the man. "No."

The woman thought back on the man's story. "What of your parents? You mentioned having a brother. Do you know if they are well?"

William shook his head. "My parents died some years back. I was informed of this through the church shortly after their passing when I was sixteen." Daniela's eyes saddened in regret, the monk continuing. "As far as my brother goes . . ." He lightly jabbed Julian in the side. "That's debatable."

The green eyes of the woman widened in realization. "You two are actual brothers then? Blood brothers, that is . . ." The two men nodded simultaneously. "I thought I saw a resemblance." She adjusted where she sat to better observe the carriage driver.

Julian cut in. "Yes, well, we may look a lot alike physically, but we have two different thoughts and opinions. William is more conservative and obedient where I'm more free-spirited and opinionated."

Daniela was further intrigued. "Oh really? What's your story then, Brother Julian?"

He snorted a laughed and met the curious green eyes of the woman peering at him from the back of the carriage. "Well, my story is nothing as respectable as Will's. It is a bit more colorful though."

"Please, do tell."

Her silent persistence through unblinking eyes brought a laugh to Julian. "All right." He resettled his focus back on the carriage-cut path and began. "Unlike my innocent and angelic baby brother, I didn't join the church at a young age nor did it to better myself. I chose to see the world and make a life for myself, exploring everything I could. Just like William stated, our family wasn't known for their riches and I knew I wouldn't get very far with that.

"So I joined a clan of gypsies when I was twelve and traveled the country. I did that for roughly six years, saving what money I could from carnivals and shows. Juggling torches on fire wasn't exactly my grand plan for life. I wanted to see more of the world and took up working on a merchant ship." A smile smeared itself across the monk's distant, almost daydreaming stare. "In just the three years I traveled with them, I saw things and places I never once imagined real. I just knew the merchant life was for me, or at least so I thought. Everything changed, however, when I found myself in Japan."

Daniela was hanging on every word the man was saying. "Japan? Why Japan? What happened?" Julian glanced down at the mesmerized green eyes and couldn't help but laugh. "Tell me, Brother, what happened?"

"I can only describe it as magic." William scoffed. Julian gave him no thought and continued telling his story. He feared if he didn't, Daniela would explode in suspense. "Everything there was like a dream made manifest. The culture, the food . . . even the lands seemed straight out of a storybook. I quit the merchant trade and decided to stay there. Ended up sort of adopted by a family there, and lived with them for the ten years I stayed there. That's when it hit me. All that time I'd been exploring, searching for the adventure I felt I was missing in life. Never occurred to me the one thing I wanted most of all was my family."

Daniela's excited smile faltered, and her heart sank in her chest. The brilliant sparkle in her eyes had been replaced with sadness. William saw this and looked away. He, too, felt his own chest tighten with emotion and wasn't about to let anyone see it.

The woman continued in question. "But you left your family."

"That I did," Julian grimly stated. "Thing is though, I didn't leave until after William went to join the church. After he left, my parents started belittling me and badgering me to join too." His jaw muscles flexed from being clenched. "It didn't seem like a family anymore and I got tired of constantly being compared to my esteemed baby brother." A heavy sigh came from the monk. "Why had I not made something more of myself when he had? So I ran away."

William cut in to continue the story from his point of view. "Then one day, eighteen years later, here comes Abbot Christophe pulling me away from my chores to reintroduce me to my *reformed* brother."

Daniela rested her attentive gaze on the forcibly composed William and furrowed her brow in confusion. "You weren't happy to see him? Especially after all that time?"

"Don't get me wrong, I was ecstatic to tears when I saw him." He paused to meet the woman's puzzled expression. "Until I realized he wasn't reformed, as he quoted to be. Because of him and his loose ethics and that *damned stick* . . ." The monk, grumbling, halted him in his storytelling. "The both of us were almost kicked from the Sect. Had it not been for Abbot Christophe, I'm sure we would've been." William's glare bore holes into the back of his brother's head.

Julian mocked, "Brother William, did I just hear a profane word come from your holy lips?"

William punched his brother in the side, blurting "Oh, be quiet." Daniela stiffened back a snicker in light of the sibling rivalry and hunkered further into her blanket. The monk grumbled and gathered his cloak and robes around him even more. "Now, if you will excuse me, I must get some rest. I've been up all night steering the carriage and need some sleep before I must do it again tonight."

The monk lay down where he had been sitting and got comfortable on the loose pile of hay beneath him. Daniela sat in silence and listened to the clomping of trotting horse hooves. This was going to be a long trip.

8

Deception

Morning gave way to early afternoon and, with it, pleasant temperatures. Though not much of a temperature increase it was still better than the piercing chill. Daniela was now sitting in the front seat next to Julian and eating pieces of bread and cheese. They chatted in whispers to themselves so as not wanting to wake William, but a loud giggle from the young woman woke him anyway.

Julian took one look at his brother and chuckled. Littered about his robes and tangled in his hair were bits of hay. "I'm not sure which has collected more hay. The wagon bed or you, Will."

The groggy monk sat up and blindly swung a hand out at the wagon driver. Though he wasn't awake enough to fully comprehend what was said, he already had a feeling it was a sarcastic comment. Julian flinched in pain from the attack and laughed, rubbing his lower back where William had hit him.

The older monk studied the other behind amused eyes cast downward over his shoulder. "So violent, Brother."

William mumbled, "Stop talking," and began dusting the pieces of hay he immediately saw off his robes.

Daniela gave Julian a partially forced "shame on you" smirk and questioned the other monk, "Would you like some bread and cheese, Brother William?"

Satisfied he had gotten as much of the hay off himself as he could, the addressed monk nodded. "That sounds good actually."

William crawled over the bench and forcibly wedged himself between Julian and the young woman, disliking how close they were seated to one another. Gladly he accepted the offered food and began eating while shooting a mischievous sneer at his brother.

As they topped a hill, the village came into view. Daniela felt relieved this part of her trip had been trouble-free. "There's the village, Brothers. We're halfway there."

Julian exclaimed, "Yes, Brother William, there's the village. Which means it's your turn to drive and I can sit in the back."

The hazel eyes of William narrowed into annoyed thin slits aimed at the older monk. Julian wasn't affected by this and only smiled in return. With a snap of the reins, the steady pace of the horse quickened to a gallop.

The wagon entered the village and pulled up to the inn, where Liam stood waving.

"Welcome back, Brothers," Liam cheerfully called. "So glad to see you two have safely arrived." He studied the young woman in the front of the wagon and broadly smiled. "And with a companion too."

William slid out of the wagon and blocked Liam's view of the woman. "Our horse, please."

Liam clapped his plump, sausage-like hands and rubbed them together. This seemed to be a thing with him. "Of course, Brothers. Allow me." He bowed to the two men and strode away, disappearing around the inn. He rushed to where a young stable boy sat, nodding off on a barrel, and shook him awake. "They're here and with the girl. Send message to the master. I wrote it, last night, and is ready for delivery."

The eyes of the stable boy widened, and he rushed to a large cage behind the stable where three courier pigeons sat on perches. He reached for the one with a small rolled-up note tied to a leg and tossed it into the air. In a rustle of feathers, the pigeon flew off.

Unknowing of the innkeeper's actions, the two monks hastily readied the borrowed horse for returning. William unbuckled the harness just as the stable boy came into view, guiding the monastery's horse. Following close behind was the still-all-too-cheerful Liam. Without delay, the monks had their returned horse harnessed and the wagon ready.

The stocky man smiled in appreciation and bowed. "I was happy to be of service."

William nodded. "The church appreciates it. God be with you, kind man."

*　　*　　*　　*

They hadn't been traveling long when Julian had a vial of ink uncorked and a piece of parchment unrolled over his lap. In his hand was a hawk feather quill that shook in his hands with each word he wrote. She wasn't sure why, but Daniela couldn't stop watching him. He seemed so peaceful and lost in his thoughts. She was curious to know what, exactly, was going through his head. She leaned back against the side wall of the wagon and glanced over to William. His eyes were downcast onto an open Bible across his hands wrapped in horse reins. Daniela figured it must've been their study time and made sure to stay quiet in respect.

*   *   *   *

Early evening started to settle over the lands and upon an abandoned village. Its streets were grown over with tall weeds and grass and its buildings dilapidated. Pale green eyes belonging to a red-haired woman peered through the cracks of a window's shutters. The familiar sound of a pigeon calling drew her curiosity. She knew this to be the much anticipated courier pigeon and watched it walk along a nearby wood railing. A small piece of parchment tied to its leg taunted her to take it. Being mindful of the sunrays shining close by, the woman carefully opened the shutters and motioned for the pigeon. The bird flew to the outstretched hand, and the woman retreated back into the shadows.

She untied the small note on its leg and started to read it. "Hmm," she hummed to herself and strode through the candlelit building. All around her, broken tables and chairs lay scattered in the interior as spiderwebs strung from the rafters.

The haunting voice of a man spoke from the shadows, startling the woman. "Something to share, my dear Valrae?"

Straightening her posture, the woman addressed as Valrae answered, "It seems like your pet innkeeper was right. The monks leaving the monastery were on a mission and not just for a routine vegetable and grain delivery." She handed the note to a blond long-haired man stepping out of the shadows. She met his cold and icy stare and continued. "They have the blood and are proceeding in return to the monastery." Valrae watched the man's eyes dart across the small scroll in his hands and questioned, "Want me to lead a group into the woods to wait for them, my Caliss?"

"No," he growled and wadded up the letter. "I already know whom I will be sending."

"But they're starving, my love! What if one of them bites her instead?" Valrae neared the man and brought a hand to his face, caressing it. "You have waited far too long for this!"

Caliss sneered a fang-bared smile and kissed the woman's hand. "Have no worries. I have been preparing this group specifically for this moment. Besides, what chance do two pathetic monks stand against four starving vampires?" He huffed a laugh at his own amusement and ran a hand through the red curls of the woman. "Tonight, I will finally have the blood for myself with my queen"—he kissed Valrae's hand again—"at my side."

* * * *

William watched the sun settle behind the horizon and sighed. "Well, there's goes the sun."

Daniela anxiously sat up from her lounging in the back of the wagon, a bit worried. "How much farther until we're there?"

Julian rolled his short staff in the hay next to him, responding, "Should be just beyond the tree line."

She grimaced upon seeing a stretch of forest growth roughly a couple miles away. "You mean, that tree line?"

William nodded. "Aye."

The woman sunk into the hay and whimpered. "Any chance we can get there before it's completely dark out?" William gave a light snap of the reins, commanding the horse to quicken its pace to a gallop.

Julian could see the worry etched in the woman's features and nudged her foot with his own. "No need to worry, my lady. Nothing will happen to you. You've got us here to protect you."

back into the bench seat and sat heavily down in an exhausted slouch. His distant gaze was unblinking.

He could see Daniela hunched down in the front floorboard and observed her from the corner of his eye. "Are you okay?"

Daniela nervously gulped and nodded her head. "I think so."

She cautiously peered over the back of the bench seat to check on the other monk. Standing over the bodies and painted in splotches of blood was Julian, holding both swords in his hands. They locked eyes, and for a moment, the young woman was intimidated. He was no longer that warm and friendly faced monk she first met at the nunnery.

Julian sheathed his swords into the other and exclaimed, "Told you we wouldn't let anything happen to you."

10

The Arrival

Panting a breath, Brother Henry wove through stone corridors and to the library. He already knew it was where the abbot would be for this was his usual reading hour. He gently pushed the door open and glanced around the spacious library. The glow from the candle flames cast an eerie light on their surroundings and along the bookshelves lining the walls.

Henry called out in a voice shaking from both the chill of the outside and from his unsettled nerves. "Abbot Christophe? Pardon my interruption, but Brothers William and Julian are almost here. There was a fire in the woods! I think . . ." His desperately searching eyes scanned the seemingly empty room, his heart beating faster. "Abbot Christophe?" The monk subconsciously reached for the cross necklace concealed beneath his robes and slipped it off his neck. Given the attack in the woods, what's to say someone didn't sneak into the monastery? With quivering hands, the monk extracted the knife crafted into the pendant. "Abbot, I think the vampires were attacking—" The sound of something moving behind the nervous monk caused him to spin around only to find no one there. "Abbot?"

The monk felt a hand capture his shoulder, and in response, he quickly spun around and prepared to attack whoever it was. But his defensive strike was quickly seized by the stronger grasp of the much older Abbot Christophe grabbing his hand. The stern, warning features of the usually peaceful man seemed distorted, causing the monk to recoil a bit.

"Easy there, Brother Henry. No need to panic." The abbot watched the monk almost collapse in fleeting panic. "You mentioned a fire in the woods?"

Henry nodded and tried to calmly explain. "That's right. The brothers were in the woods when I saw it. Brother Marcos saw it too. That's when I came to tell you. They were just coming out of the woods when I left."

"Come." Not wanting to waste any more time, Christophe guided the monk out of the library and through the hallways.

Within minutes of snaking through the stone corridors and through the church's interior, the two found themselves striding toward the monastery's heavy double oak front doors. Christophe opened one of the double oak doors just in time to see the wagon come to a halt in front of the monastery. Blood dripping in between the wooden slats of the back end startled the abbot.

Henry's mouth fell open when he saw the wagon, and he gasped upon seeing the bloody-robed Julian standing in the back. "What happened, Brothers?"

Christophe neared the wagon and stopped in his tracks when he saw the stack of bodies and collection of heads. He looked to the woman, crawling out of the front seat with the assistance of William, and questioned, "My dear, are you all right?"

Daniela nodded and released a labored breath she had been holding—for how long, she wasn't sure. "Yes, I'm fine. Just . . ." she heaved another breath and fanned the tears pooling behind the levees of her eyelids. "I need to calm down, is all."

About that time, Brother Marcos scurried outside to join the others and almost ran into the young woman in the process. He stumbled backward in an effort to prevent the collision and blurted, "My apologies," in the process. "Forgive me, my lady." His dark chocolate-brown eyes quickly darted over to the wagon, and he went motionless in shock. "Oh my G—"

Christophe barked, "Brother Marcos!" in knowing what the monk was about to say. The Spaniard timidly backed away from the religious figurehead and bit his lips together. The gray eyes of Christophe drifted up to the excited hazel eyes of Julian staring down at him, and he cocked a content smile. "And I trust you are well too, Brother?"

Julian gave a single nod of his head. "Yes, Abbot."

The much older man watched the monk slide out of the back of the wagon and open the tailgate. With a shove of his foot, the bodies fell to the ground in a series of sloshes and thuds.

William gestured to himself, stating, "I'm fine too. Thanks for asking," and scoffed.

Not meaning any discontent with Brother William, Christophe was too distracted in analyzing the bodies to pay the monk any attention.

Julian joined the kneeling abbot, questioning, "They're starving, aren't they?"

Christophe deeply frowned and nodded as he slowly rose to his feet. "Aye, that they are." His concentration rested on the assortment of heads, lifelessly staring off in different directions. "Brother Marcos, Brother Henry . . ." Both addressed men snapped their attention to the beckoning man, dreading what was about to be asked of them. "I have tasks to ask of you." Simultaneous groans came from the monks, drawing a stern stare down from the abbot. "See to it Miss Daniela's bags arrive to the guest room." Marcos and Henry exchanged relieved smiles, Christophe continuing. "Afterward, prepare a pit to burn the bodies in."

Marcos rolled his eyes, knowing there would be more to the request, and helped Henry pull aside the bloodstained blanket overlaying the leather-bound luggage. Though the luggage wasn't as bad as the blanket and the rest of the wagon bed, there were still patches of blood on them.

He scowled in having to be the bearer of bad news. "My lady . . ."

Daniela winced at the tone of voice coming from the monk and closed her eyes, shaking her head. She held up a hand to stop whatever words he was about to say next. "Don't tell me, Brother, for I already suspected as much given the mess."

Christophe cooed. "All is well, my child." He neared her and rested a gentle hand on her shoulder in comfort. He motioned for her follow him and paused just inside the doorway. He squared his gaze on the two remaining monks left without tasks. "As for you two, take the bodies where the pits are usually dug. Afterward, Brother Julian, make sure to properly dispose of the heads and, Brother William, see to it the wagon is thoroughly cleaned." The strong desire to protest the request scrolled though William's eyes. Christophe saw this. "Something you want to say, my son?"

"Must I be the one to clean the wagon, given how filthy Brother Julian already is?" He gestured to the hardly recognizable man next to him, glaring angrily in return.

Christophe's brow raised in amusement, and a smile tugged at his wrinkled features. "Then perhaps you haven't bothered to notice the back of your robes then, hmm?"

William strained to see what was being referred to and found them almost as blood soaked as his brother's. "Really, Julian? *Really?* First you throw up on them and *now this?*" Upon seeing his brother's ill fortune, Julian couldn't resist the urge to laugh, no matter how hard he tried to restrain it.

The abbot continued. "Now, see to your tasks as it is already late. The sooner you are finished, the sooner you can wash up and get something to eat."

The monks stated, "Yes, Abbot," in unison and started on their assignments.

Marcos and Henry gathered the bags between them and hustled back into the monastery to pursue the two people not far in front of them.

Christophe continued to guide the newly arrived young woman through the monastery hallways, lit by candles set in elaborate wrought-iron stands, and spoke. "At one point tomorrow, I will see to it you receive a full tour of the grounds. If it wasn't so late, I would personally escort you myself, but it is advisable you get some rest first."

Daniela nodded and stayed close to the man, slightly unnerved by the haunting chill lingering in the air and prickling at her skin. Something felt strange about this place, versus the nunnery she had stayed in, and she wasn't sure if it was good or bad. Perhaps it was only her mind in the wake of what she had just experienced toying with her judgment. Either way, she deeply inhaled a breath to calm her nerves.

Christophe could sense something was wrong and glanced at the young woman almost shoulder to shoulder with him. "Something wrong, child?"

Daniela shook her color-drained face. "Do not worry about me, Abbot. I've just been through a lot these past couple days and am worn by it. A good meal and little rest should do me well."

He could tell there was something else but didn't question it. Instead, he nodded in agreement with what the woman had said. The two people followed by Brothers Henry and Marcos exited the hallway and were back to the outside where the monastery's guesthouse sat.

Christophe paused in his strides next to a single oak door decorated with ironwork features. "This is where you will be staying." He jiggled the door's handle and lobbed a firm shoulder into the door. "The door tends to be tricky to open when it's particularly cold outside so be prepared to put a little force into it." He held it open and allowed the woman to enter. She did and found herself in the living room. A fire flickered in its hearth located on the other side of the room and bathed everything in its glow. The abbot explained, "There are four bedrooms, so feel free to choose one of your liking. I have charged Brother Julian and Brother Marcos in protecting you." He gestured to the Spanish monk entering the guesthouse. "This is Brother Marcos. He is one of my other finer combatants." The man sat the woman's belongings down on a table shy of the room's center and gave a dip of his head in greeting. "There is a tower overlooking this location and, of course, the perimeter wall surrounding the entire monastery."

Marcos exclaimed, "No matter the time of day or night, there is always going to be someone in the towers and patrolling the walls."

Daniela huffed a laugh in amazement. "Abbess Frances must be jealous. The nunnery wasn't this well-fortified."

Christophe continued to smile. "This is one of the Sect's most secured locations."

Daniela found the guesthouse very pleasing. She had been used to staying in the dormitory with the nuns, so a guesthouse of this size was quite different. Henry entered the house next and joined the bags on the table with his own load.

Christophe studied the fire and was displeased on how low it had become. "Brother Marcos, please see to the fire before leaving."

Daniela cut in, knowing the monk already had something else to do. "It's fine, Abbot, I can do it. I'm used to tending to fires, and besides, Brother Marcos already has enough to do after this."

Christophe's slimmed gaze shifted between the young woman and the Spaniard, and he nodded. "Very well then, my child. I will leave you to your privacy." After the two monks left the room, the abbot followed and shut the door behind him.

11

Something to Think About

William grumbled and splashed a bucket of water into the bloody wagon bed. "Why am I always the one having to clean up your messes?" Meanwhile, Julian stuffed two of the four heads into a burlap sack.

Julian tied up the first bag and set it to the side, against a stable post. "Because you're lucky, I guess?"

William picked up a broom leaning against the front bench seat and started sweeping the blood-soaked hay out of the back end. "I wouldn't call it lucky, Brother." In his sweeping away a pile of hay, he came across one of the severed hands. "For crying out loud, will you do something with this?"

The scolded monk peered over the wagon bed side and saw the hand lying among the hay. He snickered. "Need a hand with that?"

William clenched his jaw in aggravation and tried to refrain from losing his temper. Julian crawled into the wagon bed to retrieve the hand and kicked around the hay for the second hand he knew was lying around somewhere. When he found it, he jumped out and tossed them into the second bag he had lying on the ground.

The sweeping monk continued his task. "I know one thing though. Should you be stupid enough and attempt anything with Miss Daniela, I won't lie for you to clean up any messes you make."

Julian shoved a third head into the burlap sack and responded, "What makes you think I'd attempt anything?"

Both men didn't notice the silent shadow creeping across the ground toward them. William resumed his conversation with the other man.

"Don't try and play innocent with me, Brother. I know you better than that and have seen the way you've been looking at her."

"Brothers . . .," came the eerily calm voice of Abbot Christophe behind them. He wore a sly smile across his shadow-sculpted features.

Julian stood up to meet the observing gray eyes of the black-robed figure and nodded in acknowledgment. "Abbot."

William gave his brother a cautious stare before turning his attention to the addressing man behind him. "Abbot Christophe. Something you need?"

The older man strode around the front wagon, avoiding the bloody water pooling under the bed, and spoke. "I came to check on your progress." His gaze fell on the charred head sitting on the ground and getting dripped on by water seeping through the cracks of the wagon. "Which reminds me. Brother Henry mentioned seeing a fire in the woods. I'm guessing it is safe to assume this"—he nudged the head with a foot—"is the reason why?"

Julian quickly grabbed the head by its matted hair and stuffed it into the sack. "That would be Brother William's fire breathing, Abbot. He saved my life."

Intrigued, the religious figurehead shifted his stare to the further annoyed monk and arched a brow. "Is this correct, my son?"

William gave a glower to his brother and answered the abbot's question. "Yes, Abbot, it is."

"And all this time, I was under the impression you had no interest in Brother Julian's 'bad habits' as you've so described them numerous times." He huffed an amused laugh at the angry, flustered monk. Julian stood up, curious to know how his brother would answer.

"I'm not, Abbot." The barely tethered patience was evident in William's tone of voice. "But when constantly around someone practicing them, it's a bit hard to *not* pick up a thing or two."

Christophe's smile broadened. "Not all *bad habits* are as bad as you think, dear boy. After all, it killed a vampire and saved your brother and, quite possibly, Miss Daniela too." William's sour countenance melted with realization, and he locked gazes with the powerful eyes of the priest. "Hmm?" The monk sighed and resumed his sweeping away the clumps of bloody hay out of the wagon bed.

Julian's chest tightened with pride for his brother, and he faintly smiled to himself. He gathered the bloody burlap sacks in his hands and politely excused himself. "Excuse me, Abbot, I need to take these to the pits to be burned."

Christophe called to the monk striding away, "Bother Julian, I advise you keep your weapon with you, especially in light of the attacks earlier."

unnatural chill of the touch startling Julian. "Remember that and not falter to weakness, but stand strong against it."

Julian bowed his head in acknowledgment of his mentor's words and responded, "Yes, Abbot."

Christophe patted the man on the shoulder and forced another weary smile. "Now, go get cleaned up and please get rid of those robes." He studied the dried patches of blood scattered along the sleeves and streaking down the front. "They are not worth salvaging. Brother William's as well."

"Yes, Abbot." But when he started walking away, Christophe calling out stopped him yet again.

"And, Brother Julian . . ." The monk glancing over his shoulder to the figurehead urged the older man to continue. "Keep your weapon close to you. I do not wish to take any chances of something happening to Miss Daniela should you be unarmed."

A pleased smile cut across Julian's face, and subconsciously, he tightened his grip around his treasured swords. "Consider it done." The monk proudly strode away and through the corridors to the bathhouse.

In his striding to the bathhouse, Julian found himself distracted in thought as he failed to acknowledge a novitiate addressing him with concern. It startled the wide-eyed teenage novitiate seeing the monk's robe covered in blood, and he stood aside, allowing Julian to pass by without a word. Since their return, word had quickly spread throughout the monastery of what had happened. There was much speculation on the real details of what happened, but very little explanation. The novitiate's bewildered gawk then fell on the blood-caked short staff carried by the older man, and he became further curious. Apparently, the conjectures made by the other monks weren't too far off from being right, especially given the present appearance of the usually clean Julian.

By the time the monk had arrived to his destination, he had left a trail of strange stares and curious whispers in his wake throughout the monastery. William fell silent in his conversing with Marcos and Henry as soon as Julian entered the room. Everyone could see something different in his eyes. Was it something Abbot Christophe had said? Was it the realization of how serious things had just become, what with the vampires openly attacking now?

Not a word was said between the men while they washed off.

Julian discarded his robes to the floor to expose his blood-smeared body beneath. William became startled by this. Was his brother injured at one point, and he didn't disclose it? How much of that blood belonged to the vampires and how much to the man?

William questioned in genuine worry, "Are you hurt, Brother?"

Julian shook his head and leaned his sheathed swords against a nearby wooden tub. "Other than my face hurting, no."

Marcos gave an uncertain sideways glance at the soiled monk. "Sure looks like a lot of blood from starving vampires."

Julian retrieved a nearby linen washcloth off a wooden rack mounted on the wall and calmly sat down in the tub full of steaming water. He took a moment to lounge back and let the warmth set into his cold body. All around his form, blood washing off him started to turn the water pink. When he moved, his body ached in protest as he ran handfuls of water over his face and head. To make sure he was getting all the blood off, he scrubbed at his skin and swished the water-soaked rag around in his hair.

The three silent monks then watched Julian unsheath his swords and meticulously clean them with the washrag. Not wanting to stick around and endure more of the disturbing scene, William, Marcos, and Henry got dressed and left the bathhouse.

Julian could still feel the sensation of his blades slicing through flesh and bone, and it scared him. During his fighting the vampires, what happened to him? What had he let himself become? Though he knew how to fight with his swords and was prepared to do so when needed, he had never used them to kill until the attack in the woods. With the wiping of the rag along the blade's edge, Julian could see his reflection. Was this the beginning of things to come? He closed his eyes and leaned his head against his hand tightly gripping a sword's handle and prayed Abbot Christophe was right.

The troubled monk wasn't sure how long he had sat there, whispering his prayers to himself. By now, the water had lost its heat. Grumbling, he sheathed his swords and got dressed. Hopefully it wasn't too late for his share of dinner leftovers. The monk wasn't sure if Daniela had eaten yet or not and went to the guesthouse, gently knocking on the door.

Daniela stirred from a nap she had unintentionally fallen into, curled up in front of the fireplace, and glanced over to the door. Another knock came, and Daniela rubbed her sleep-heavy eyes, asking, "Yes?"

Julian's voice came from the other side of the door. "My lady, my apologies for disturbing you, but I was on my way to get dinner and wasn't sure if you had already eaten or not."

Daniela tried to open the door and grumbled. "No, I haven't. I was going to earlier, but . . ." She wrenched backward on the door handle in frustration. "Couldn't open the door, of all things, so I decided to pass."

"Clear the door." The man wasn't sure if the woman was near it or not, but he didn't want to take any chances. He shoved his entire body weight into the door and almost stumbled inward when it gave way. "Are you okay?"

Daniela nodded and rewrapped her cloak around her for warmth against the chill of the air invading through the open door. "I should be asking you the same thing."

The man subtly smiled under the alluring gaze of the woman's green eyes—for why, he wasn't sure. "Would you like to join me for dinner then?" His smile broadened seeing her nod in acceptance.

13

Weapon of Choice

After dinner, Daniela allowed herself to be guided back to the guesthouse by the armed Marcos and Julian. All three were glad to be within the house, despite the once cozy fire being reduced to smoldering coals. The room was void of firelight, but the glow from the coals still provided some luminance.

Marcos propped his spear against the center table in exchange for the hearth's stoker and began stirring the coals. The young woman ran her fingers along the weapon's smooth wood shaft and to the polished spear tip. She traced the etched accents with a finger and tapped the very tip with her thumb. "This is your weapon of choice, I presume?"

The spear's owner nodded. "That's right."

Her eyes scanned the polished wooden surface and midway metal band for any trick gimmicks. "Does it do anything neat? Like how Brother Julian's stick is actually two swords?"

Marcos chuckled and shook his head. "No. See, unlike Brother Julian, I prefer real skill to use my weapon."

Julian sat against a wall on the floor with legs crossed. In his lap was one of his unsheathed swords as he worked on sharpening the dual-bladed weapon with a whetstone. "Excuse me, but my weapons do require *real* skill."

Daniela could see an argument, while playful, starting to form between the brothers and changed the subject off their weapons. "Other than you two being primarily in charge of my safety, who else will be protecting me?"

Marcos sneered at the other monk and answered, "Several actually." He brought a more serious gawk on the young woman. "Those who are more combat experienced will continuously patrol the perimeter throughout the night in shifts. Brothers Peter, David, Garret, and Luke will swap in patrolling the immediate vicinity outside the house." He reached for a log on top of a stack near the fireplace and tossed it onto the grate. Sparks erupted into the air and up through the chimney. "After the attack in the woods tonight, Abbot Christophe is taking no chances should they try and attack the monastery."

Julian spoke next. "Just before your transfer, the church's Sect division had reinforcements reassigned here for precautionary measure."

Daniela took a seat at the table, confused. "Why not just send them to the nunnery? I was already there and wouldn't that have been better than transferring me out in the open? And in a wagon cart, no less. Why was I being transported in a wagon cart anyway, and not a carriage with armed escorts?" She saw the slightly offended gaze of hazel eyes beneath lowered brows aim right at her. "No offense, Brother." He shrugged and resumed sharpening his swords.

Marcos explained the best he could. "To prevent suspicions. It's not uncommon for Abbot Christophe to have us disseminate grains, vegetables, and meats to local settlements unable to fully support their own. We always transport the supplies in the wagon with two monks. Brother William is almost always one of those traveling."

"Why him?"

Chocolate eyes met curious green ones. "He's a physician and sometimes, there are sick needing tending to in one of the towns." The Spanish monk returned to busying himself with the gradually growing fire. "To answer your question on why the Sect didn't send reinforcements to the nunnery is because the nunnery is much smaller and far less secure than the monastery. You were sent there because it's more off the beaten path than here. The Sect thought you stood a greater chance of not being found if off in the country." He snorted. "Guess not."

Julian ran a thumb along one of the sharpened blades to gauge his work. "I advise you get some rest, my lady. Morning service comes quite early and the day only gets busier from there."

She nodded in agreement. "I am a bit sleepy. It's best you kind souls do the same." Daniela gathered her leather bags off the table and carried them to a room located toward the back of the guesthouse. "Good night, Brothers."

Satisfied the logs were as good as they were going to get, Marcos slowly got up. He retrieved his spear and, too, selected a room for himself. He chose one of the more forward-located rooms should he need to act quickly in case of an attack. His dark eyes gave a final observation of the other monk, relocating himself to sit before the fire. There was sadness in those normally carefree eyes, and it bothered the Spaniard.

"Try to get some sleep, Brother," Marcos stated and disappeared into his new room.

Julian didn't pause or look up from his work. He needed to do something to help clear the scrambled thoughts in his head, and now was the perfect time to do it. Everything was quiet and he away from the distractions and prying eyes of the other monks in the dormitory. Thinking on that, he briefly hesitated in his blade sharpening to give a quick glance at Daniela's closed bedroom door. The thought of something potentially bad happening to her, as it could've today, greatly unnerved him. He might've allowed his defenses to slip once, but he wasn't about to make that same mistake again. If only William knew just how grateful he was for his saving him.

*　　*　　*　　*

Valrae stood aside and watched Caliss tear through the old house's interior. Chairs were thrown and empty bookshelves turned over. He roared into the dim candlelit night air in rage. She scoffed. "I knew I should've led the team myself."

Caliss snarled another roar and slammed a fist into a wall. The boards splintered on impact and sent slivers of wood into the infuriated man's knuckles. He couldn't care less and studied the blood trickling from the open wounds. "That bastard of a monk would have killed you too."

Valrae hissed in offense to the statement. "Hardly! I'm not like those pathetic weaklings you let run amok!" She watched the temper-flared man pull a splinter out of his hand. "I am stronger than them and not to mention a lot smarter. Had I have been there, I would've taken out that horse! No mortal stands a chance outrunning one of us!" Seeing him paying her no attention, she brought a hand under his jaw to force his eyes on her. "Let me lead the team next time. You know I won't let you down."

Caliss jerked her hand away from his face with his uninjured one and harshly grabbed his jaw with his bloody one. He bore his fangs inches from her face and growled, "You will do what I tell you." His tightening grip brought a whimper from the redheaded woman. "Do not question my orders and decisions." He tossed the woman backward and away from his immediate view.

Valrae growled and wiped away at the wetness on her jaw and cheek. She looked to her fingers to see his blood shimmer in the candlelight and licked it. Her pale green eyes grew bloodshot the longer she watched the vampire lord pluck the remaining slivers of wood from his hand. When the last one hit the floor, she sauntered over to him.

She began, "You call it questioning your orders. I call it guaranteeing your success." The vampiress ran a finger along the top of the man's injured hand and lightly snorted. "Despite your being the Lady Lilith's favored child, you can't do everything by yourself." Valrae retracted her now blood-covered finger and licked at the crimson liquid. "I am only here to serve you, my lord." She took a step closer to him and whispered into his ear, "But how can I help you, when you won't let me?"

Their eyes locked, and Caliss lightly growled in response. "You do realize your accompanying the next team would send you into the monastery . . ." Valrae cocked a brow and teased a smile. "You're no match for Christophe. The fool might be weakened on holy ground, but make no mistake of his strength."

The woman huffed a laugh. "That's what the rest of the team is for. They're expendable. Let them die for the greater good. I'll have them distract the old man and I'll personally go for the bitch myself."

"You will not hurt her."

Valrae lowered her gaze on the man. "My dear Caliss, have you no trust in me anymore?"

"When the time is right, I will personally go for the girl myself." He caressed the woman's face with the back of his injured hand, painting her cheek with the residual damp blood. "All I need you to do is get me a sample of her blood." Caliss turned away from the vampiress and started licking his hand clean. "Before I risk everything, I want to make sure her blood will still yield the desired effects."

Valrae crossed her hands over her chest. "And if she doesn't?"

"I'll have her bled dry and her body burned along with those ignorant fools in the monastery." His bloodshot blue eyes met the woman's irritated pale green ones. "If I can't have her blood, then no one will."

This was not what she wanted to hear. A part of her very much wanted the blood for herself. If it wasn't for Caliss's already superior power granted from the Lady Lilith, as well as his already being empowered from a previous blood consumption centuries prior, she'd chance taking it for herself. "Very well then. When do you plan on attacking? I can assemble a team tonight."

"No!" Caliss barked out. "Christophe will undoubtedly have the monastery on high alert after tonight's . . . failure." A low growl emanated from his throat. "No, as much as it angers me, we must wait. Wait for their defenses to slacken. Let them think all is well and when the time is right . . ." His bare feet slowly closed the distance between himself and Valrae. "Then you and your little pets can go play."

"Just give me the word, my lord, and I will be ever at your service."

Caliss stopped just shy of contacting the woman's lips with his own and whispered, "As you should be."

14

A Matter of Skill

Days turned into weeks. Without realizing it, three weeks had passed. Time went by quickly at the monastery, between tending to the livestock and assisting with the vegetable garden when not studying or in prayer service. For the combat-trained monks, they had two times set aside during the day for training. It was during these sessions Daniela got to see the extent of their abilities. They held nothing back when practicing either armed or unarmed. Their quick and precise movements were hypnotizing to watch.

Julian used two sparring sticks in place of his swords so as not to involuntarily injure someone. Marcos kept to his spear, and Brother Henry completely surprised Daniela when revealing his particular knack for throwing knives. They varied in sizes and were kept in either custom-made wrist guards or a thin leather belt.

One of the newest and youngest of the monks, a novitiate and teen named Jordan, preferred archery. His shots weren't always exactly on the targets' bull's-eye, but they were still respectably clustered together. If this same pattern applied to a living target, the shots would no doubt be lethal.

On seldom occasion Abbot Christophe would oversee the training. He would provide pointers to the brothers where he could, and none questioned him. Everyone knew he was one of the Sect's best and a skilled combatant. The abbot's past was something never spoken of, which brought curiosity to the monks. How many vampires had he slain? Had he ever seen any major battles against some of the more threatening ones? Very rarely had the abbot ever actually picked up a weapon and practice with the monks.

When he did, the rest of the monks would stand aside to watch greatness at its finest.

Today was one of those days. Christophe strode out onto the shady section of the lawn where the monks practiced, with a sheathed broadsword in his hand. Immediately the several pairs of sparring monks paused in their training to study the figurehead. Who would be chosen for today's unexpected tutorial?

He stood there, hands folded before him and resting on the decorative butt of his sword's hilt. His gray eyes shifted between the many alert faces aimed in his direction. Even those who were working the vegetable garden halted their work to observe the unfolding scene.

"Brother Marcos," the abbot called.

The Spaniard approached the addressing man, spear in hand. "Yes, Abbot?"

Christophe never took his unblinking watch off the monk when sliding his sword out of its sheath. He handed the empty scabbard to Jordan, standing nearby, and gave a nod to the man standing a few feet from him. "Care to entertain an old man in a duel?"

The brown eyes of the monk sparkled in a rush of excitement. "It would be my honor, sir."

"Good." Both men took a ready stance with the side of their blades pointed upward and touching. Christophe held his sword with his right hand while his left was held behind him. "Begin," and the match started.

Before Marcos could do anything, Christophe used his sword to push the spear aside. Then, using his left hand, he pushed his opponent's weapon aside by its upper plate guard. This allowed him to safely close the distance between him and the other with his sword at Marcos's neck.

The Spaniard could feel the blade's edge lightly rake across his throat and arched a brow in surprise. "Okay, so you're going to play that way, are you?"

Christophe lowered his sword and smirked, taking a step back. "I wasn't aware there was a certain way to 'play.'"

Marcos took his own steps back to further add distance. "Let's try this again."

"Very well." This time, Christophe held his blade outstretched for maximum distance. He grinned at his opponent in a subtly arrogant way, taunting him.

When he lunged toward the monk, Marcos briefly released his spear's handle with his left hand to now grip it with the tip aimed to the ground. His own lunge forward and swift jab downward had his blade against the abbot's forwardmost knee.

Christophe felt the contact and shifted his gaze downward. "Very good."

For the third match, Marcos almost got another attack past the abbot, had it not been for the sword's sharp bite nicking his right side.

Marcos took a step back to analyze the injury and saw a shallow cut peek through the tear in his robes.

Christophe smirked. "Don't tell me you can't keep up with someone as old as me?"

Several snickers came from the gathered spectators, Marcos scoffing. "Abbot, with much due respect, in the years you have been walking this world since God brought forth the sun, you have had much time to practice."

The much older man laughed at the comment. "I'm not that old, dear boy. Much to the belief of many, I wasn't around when . . . God brought forth the sun."

"Almost though, right?"

Christophe gave a lowered, cocked smile to the monk and pressed on with the duel.

When one or the other would land a successful attack on the other, the monks would cheer. Marcos made sure to hold back his strikes so as not to injure the monastery overseer. The sun was shy of peeking over the monastery walls, Henry taking note of this. He rushed to the abbot's side and whispered something in his ear the others could not hear.

The figurehead nodded in understanding and patted Henry the monk on his shoulder. "Thank you for reminding me, Brother. I had almost forgotten." Christophe motioned for Jordan to hand him back his scabbard and sheathed his blade. "Thank you, Brother Marcos, for the much needed distraction and . . . entertainment."

His smile stretching from ear to ear deepened the wrinkles in his face. It was a smile the brothers hadn't seen in a very long time, and it was refreshing to see.

The Spaniard gave a bow in respect. "The pleasure was all mine, Abbot."

Christophe turned and left the training grounds, Henry at his heels.

* * * *

William dabbed a warm, wet cloth on one of many cuts riddling Marcos's bare upper body. The man hissed and jerked away from the unwanted sting of the water. William sighed. "Hold still so I can analyze you."

Julian giggled at the other man behind his eating an apple, Marcos scoffing. "For someone as old as him, I'm surprised he's still got a lot of fight in him. Shouldn't his joints be stiffening or something?" He almost lurched off the monastery's infirmary bed after William pressed into one of the more tender cuts. "You did that on purpose!"

The physician scorned. "My apologies."

Julian swallowed his bite and gave his own comment. "What were you saying a while back? You preferred real skill to use your weapon?"

Marcos rolled his eyes and laughed to himself. "How about next time, you be Abbot Christophe's sparring partner . . . That way, I can laugh at you getting carved up."

"I know better than that," Julian smarted off, taking another bite of his apple.

The three men's conversing was interrupted by a monk sporting red hair and brown eyes. William saw him and the look of urgency on his face. "Something I can help you with, Brother Matthew?"

The newly arrived clasped his hands before him and nodded. "Brothers, my apologies for interrupting, but night is soon approaching. Abbot Christophe finds it best you come to dinner as soon as you can before patrols begin at sundown."

The others nodded in understanding, and Matthew scampered back out of the infirmary. Marcos's watch remained in the direction Matthew had gone in. "I don't know what it is about that man. Something about him always seems strange. He's always mousing around the monastery, doing who knows what."

William tossed the dirty rag aside and collected another clean one off a nearby table. "He's one of the monastery's groundskeepers. What's so strange about that?"

The Spaniard shrugged, shaking his head.

15

Uninvited Guests

The pale green eyes of Valrae slimmed in their following Caliss pacing in front of the house's empty fireplace. Both hands' fingertips drummed against the other's in thought. He stopped to study the motionless and impatient woman. "Bring me the sample of the girl's blood."

The woman deviously smiled. "As you wish . . . my lord . . ." She briskly strode out into the chill of the night and stood, observing the gloomy figures lurking where the moonlight dared not touch. Two men could be seen standing side by side beneath a stable overhang. "You two . . ." Valrae's attention shifted to a tall man with long greasy black hair emerging out of a burned-down house. "And you . . . with me."

The tall man stood almost toe to toe with the woman and gawked down at her much smaller frame. "What do ask of me, my lady?" When he spoke, his breath reeked of rotted flesh.

Valrae cocked a sinister grin and trained down her gaze. "You take care of the guard detail protecting the blood."

The vampire snarled. "What of the old man?"

"That's where they come in." Valrae looked over to the two walking up to join the first. "You"—she gestured to the smaller of the two, caked in mud, and continued—"I want you to infiltrate the monastery and create as much chaos as you can." She shot her attention to the third. "Your job is to thin as many of the monastery's forces as you can. I don't care what you do to do it. Just see it gets done. The less of them roaming about the better." Her arms crossed over her chest. "Feel free to feast yourselves on whomever you want, but leave the girl to me."

The three nodded and ran off into the woods near the village ruins. Valrae shot Caliss an over-the-shoulder wink and pursued the three men in a casual stride.

*   *   *   *

Marcos paused in his patrolling the perimeter wall to watch the moon and leaned against his spear. In just a few hours, it would be sunrise. His stomach growled the more his mind hovered over the thought of breakfast soon approaching, and he sighed. His gaze drifted over to the guesthouse very near where he was taking guard. Everything was quiet as it had been all evening. His attention then shifted over in the opposite direction where the monastery's apple trees were near the vegetable garden. Would anyone notice if he took one of the ripe apples, he felt distantly calling to him, for a quick snack? That would require him leaving his post, and he didn't feel comfortable with that.

He was taken off guard, however, when the voice of a monk called behind him. Marcos turned around to face David, a stocky and lively bearded monk in his late twenties. Though he seemed quite harmless, anyone who knew him would say otherwise. Beneath his sleeves he wore leather armbands where knives were safely tucked away. It was often a question to others when wondering how many other knives he had concealed on him. Between him and Henry, there was no short supply of throwing weapons.

Marcos commented, "I wasn't aware you were on patrol duty tonight."

David's plump cheeks further puffed out in a smile. "I'm covering for Brother Luke. He wasn't feeling well after dinner tonight."

Marcos gave a slow nod. "Brother Henry's meatloaf tends to do that to people, especially if people don't—" An indistinguishable person sneaking around stopped him in midsentence. "I just saw someone poking around between the abbot's house and business rooms."

David glanced over his shoulder in the direction the other man was watching. "Should I alert someone?"

The Spaniard's eyes didn't falter from their watch. The form emerged from their momentary hiding to run toward the infirmary and disappear again. "Ring the bell. I think we're about to have some uninvited guests."

David gathered his robes from around his feet and quickly dashed toward the bell tower.

Marcos knew he needed to warn Abbot Christophe and Brother Julian of the possible attack. Soon the bell would ring, and everyone in the monastery would know a possible threat was present. In the meantime, he kept his eyes forward and alert on the spans of wheat field beyond the perimeter wall and forest edge.

A moment later, the bell boisterously chiming shattered the quiet air. Between rings, David yelled in warning, "Intruder! Intruder in the monastery!"

No sooner had he just fallen asleep than Julian was jerked awake by the bell ringing. Was it time for morning service already? He sat up and rubbed his eyes, noticing the house still warm. Had Daniela gotten up during the night and tended to the fire? He exited his room to find Daniela doing the same in equal confusion.

She yawned out, "It's too early for morning service, isn't it?"

Julian shook his head. "That's not the bell for morning service."

Frantic pounding came at the door and startled both people. William burst into the room, wide-eyed and panic-stricken. "There's an intruder in the monastery!"

Julian's attention shot to the terrified young woman. "Stay here and lock the door behind me." He grabbed his sheathed twin swords he had lying on the bed and followed his brother out of the guesthouse. "Do *not* answer the door unless it is myself or Abbot Christophe, understand?"

The woman nodded and nervously watched both monks leave. She forcefully shut the door behind them by throwing her body weight into it. Her trembling fingers were barely able to click the lock over, and she backed away from it in terror. Her mind was racing in fear of worst-case scenarios.

Marcos could be heard yelling, "Take refuge or take arms, Brothers! Quickly!"

Julian charged up the perimeter wall's stairs, both swords extracted, and searched the focused expression of the Spaniard. "How many?"

"Just the one that I saw." Marcos looked to and pointed in the direction of the abbot's house. "I saw it run that way and then disappear somewhere around the infirmary."

A flicker of movement from the hay field startled them, Julian's eyes widening. A lofty and grungy man came running toward the two monks from the concealment of the hay. In a powerful lunge, the creature leapt into the air.

"Watch out!" Julian pushed Marcos to the ground as the vampire landed on top of the wall next to them.

Julian slashed the intruder's upper arm reaching out to grab him with one sword and then across his side with his other blade. The vampire roared out in pain and balled up a fist, landing a concussive blow to the monk's face. Julian was made unconscious and sent to the hard stone ground with a thud.

Marcos striking the offender in the gut with his spear had little effect in stopping the attacker. If anything, it made him that much more angrier. Any further actions were halted by an abnormally strong grip taking hold of the spear just below the blade and jerking its owner off the perimeter wall.

The doors of the abbot's house erupted open, giving way to the man's exit with his sword in hand. His wide gray eyes instantly went to the guesthouse and up to the perimeter wall not far from him. He could see Julian lying motionless on the wall and feared the worst. He rushed to the stairs where he saw Marcos lying on the ground nearby.

Christophe went to the man to see if he was still alive. "Brother Marcos?" He gave a firm shake and noticed the monk holding his side. "Are you all right?"

Panting for air, the Spaniard wheezed in answer. "I think so. I only got thrown off the perimeter wall."

"Can you stand? *Can you still fight?*" Marcos got to his feet with the assistance of Christophe and grimaced.

"I've felt better, but I can still fight."

"Good." The abbot bent down to pick up the man's spear and shoved it into his chest for him to take. "Find the demon and make sure it's dead! You know what to do."

The monk nodded and gave a weak glance up the wall. "Brother Julian . . ."

An explosion from somewhere across the monastery got the abbot's attention. "I'll check on him. Just *go!*"

The abbot ran up the stairs and to the monk starting to come to. Julian reached for his swords and weakly stood up, still slightly dizzy from getting hit. "Vampires . . . they're here . . . I need to get to Daniela."

He barely heard Christophe order, "Stay with the blood," over the ringing in his ears and nodded. In a flash of black robes, the abbot was gone.

16

Defending the Blood

Daniela shrieked and leapt back where she had been standing, staring wide-eyed at the door. Something was trying to get in, and she feared it not being any of the monastery monks. Still, she did as told and refrained from opening the door. Another collision rattled its hinges, and she feared if help didn't come soon, the door would be broken through.

Julian guided himself down the stairs with the assistance of leaning against the wall and came close to falling toward the bottom stairs. He could hear the guesthouse door impacted and rounded the building's front to find his attacker trying to get in.

The monk aimed a sword at the aggressor. "I don't like getting hit in the face. Bad . . . bad idea." He was determined to find a way to make the vampire's head hurt just as much as, if not more than, his head at the present time.

Another rush into the door loosened the top hinges. The vampire let out a wail and fled the guesthouse door. Forgetting his order to stay with Daniela, Julian followed the sprinting vampire into the torch-lit hallway leading to the clerical guest chambers. Luckily they were empty, unlike two weeks ago.

Anxious and anticipating an encounter, Julian slowly crept along the wall and in the direction leading to the scriptorium. He could hear echoes of a woman's laughter and knew it wasn't Daniela's. There had to be a third vampire somewhere within the monastery, but he wasn't sure where it was coming from. Whispering voices and a breath of cold air came from

---

behind the monk. This unnerved the man, and he spun around to find no one there.

The monk deeply inhaled a calming breath and resumed his examining every room within the corridor. He thought he saw movement in one of the rooms only to find it bring a tapestry swinging on its nail in a draft.

Julian tightened his grip on his swords and proceeded to the next room when echoes of a woman's scream flooded the monk's ears. His attention shot to the hallway door leading outside to the guesthouse, and he froze in panic.

Realization hit him. This was just a distraction to lure him away from the young woman. The door's hinges were already weakened, and it wouldn't take any vampire much effort to completely break it down. Why didn't he think of that sooner?

Julian ran outside and bellowed, "Daniela!"

He could see the front door partially open and didn't hesitate to barge his way in. His heart seized in his chest, and his jaw instantly clenched. Firelight from the hearth highlighted the tear-filled eyes of Daniela restrained in the clutches of Valrae. The young woman whimpered against the vampire's grasp.

Dribbles of blood from a fresh cut ran down the young woman's neck and onto the vampire's hand around her throat. She inhaled the enticing scent and purred. "Here I was thinking tales of the blood being like that of sweet honey a lie." She sneered. "I wonder if she tastes as good as she smells."

Julian slowly stepped toward the two people, thinking of ways to kill the vampire without harming Daniela in the process.

Daniela could feel the vampire's fangs brush against her neck and choked a desperate cry. Icy cold fingers void of all life gently caressed her face along her cheekbone. Valrae spoke in a hushed voice. "Might want to stop right there, monk."

Valrae ran her long clawlike fingernails through Daniela's hair and collected a handful at the back of her head. Jerking back fully exposed the neck vein pulsing with the young woman's rapid heartbeat. The frightened woman could see Julian's eyes burning with rage. Movement visible over the monk's shoulder got her attention, and her eyes widened in fear.

The man shifted his eyes to the side and flexed his grip on both of his swords. He had suspected he was being hunted and quickly turned around, swinging one of his swords behind him. The vampire he had previously been following was back. The creature dodged the attack and grabbed Julian's face with a hand drenched in fresh blood. Paralyzing pain shot through the monk's jaw, and the vampire's mouth curled into a just as blood-soaked sneer.

The monk swung a sword at the attacker only to find his hand restrained by his captor's much stronger one. The vampire released a mocking laugh and head butted the monk, causing Julian to be momentarily dazed again. The voice of Daniela yelling his name bore through the ringing in his ears, and he forced what composure he could over himself. He struggled to get his arm free, but his wrist was painfully twisted.

Julian cried out and dropped his sword to the floor from a failing grip.

Behind him, Valrae laughed and stated to Daniela, "Looks like your fearless protector isn't so strong after all, is he?"

Julian wasn't about to let things happen like this and, in swift thinking, spit in the grungy vampire's eye. This allowed a brief second's distraction the monk took advantage of. He took the sword in his unbound hand and ran it completely through the vampire's skull from under the chin.

The merciless grip released Julian's face, allowing him to shove the sword farther through the vampire's skull. "Now you know how my head feels," the monk growled out and slammed the man into a wall behind him.

Jerking the dual-edged blade toward him split the other's lower face open. Blood from the vampire surged onto Julian as the monk felt the grasp on his right hand break free. He swapped sword hands and slashed at his opponent's neck. Blood splattered across the brick wall and doused the monk even more. Three good hacks from the blade completely severed the head from the rest of the body.

Valrae's ear-piercing screech caused the monk to turn around and face the livid vampire. His hazel eyes stood out against the blood running down his face. There was a barely tethered madness within those eyes, and Daniela shuddered at the sight.

Julian pointed the tip of his sword at Valrae and growled, "Release her." The vampire snarled a hiss and harshly tossed Daniela to the ground. Without removing his acidic, blood-drenched stare from the vampire, he ordered the young woman, "Get to your room and take cover."

Daniela couldn't take her eyes off the nightmarish monk and ran to her room, slamming the door closed. The fang-bared vampire flexed her hand on which Daniela's blood had dripped on and scoffed. Her eyes darted to a bucket of water near the fireplace and kicked it over, into the fire.

Coals sizzled in being extinguished, flooding the house with smoke and darkness. Whispers of movement came from beside the monk, and abruptly, he slashed a sword into the cold breeze. Painful cries of the vampire filled his ears. Knowing he had impelled the woman with his blade, he hoisted the blade upward into the woman's torso.

Valrae grabbed the front of the monk's robe and slashed across his chest with her clawlike nails. Following suit a second later were his own cries as a paralyzing pain overcame his chest. The vampire took hold of his neck and pushed him away from her, extracting the blade from her gut. Not wanting to stick around, and having what she came for dried onto her hand, the vampire fled the guesthouse.

Valrae's laughter filled the chaotic monastery air, but her celebrating didn't last long. She was almost to the perimeter wall in escape when a sharp jolt of pain tore into her hip. Her leg collapsed beneath her weight, and she shrieked out, crashing to the ground. Her bloodshot eyes looked to the source of the pain to see a crossbow's bolt buried deep in her hip.

She hissed and snapped her attention upward to see a teenage monk load another bolt into a crossbow. Coming up on his right was Christophe. "Excellent shot, Brother Jordan."

Jordan snorted a laugh. "You were right about the crossbow, Abbot. It offers a lot more penetration!"

Valrae yanked the silver-tipped bolt out of her bloody thigh and threw it to the ground. She rose to her feet and laughed maniacally. "Abbot Christophe! What a pleasure to see you! . . . Again," she growled out more seriously.

The abbot slowly approached her with his sword held close to him. "Lady Valrae. My apologies for not feeling the same."

Jordan fired another shot, but his target narrowly avoided it by leaping onto the perimeter wall and disappearing over it.

Christophe knew she had come from the guesthouse and hurried to it in concern for its occupants. He gasped when he saw the sight within.

17

In the Aftermath

Julian groaned and grabbed the burning in his chest. His breathing was labored and body breaking out in a cold sweat. Every time he tried to at least sit up, he was sent back to the floor in waves of nausea washing over him. He could hear the faint voice of Daniela call to him, and her fear-stricken face filled his view. She still sounded so distant and inaudible like he was trying to hear her underwater.

Daniela cried at being lost on what to do. She could see the slashes across his chest beneath his torn robe and further panicked.

Abbot Christophe shouted to the young woman, "Miss Daniela! Are you all right? Were you bitten?"

The woman hysterically nodded. "I'm fine, but Brother Julian is hurt!"

"May I enter?" When there wasn't an immediate answer from the woman, he questioned again more sternly, "May I enter?" Daniela looked to him in perplexity. Why would he ask her something like that? She suddenly became aware she was still wearing her nightgown and blushed.

He must be asking for modesty's sake. "Of course, yes, anything, just help him, *please*!"

"What happened?" Christophe joined her side and pushed her out of the way to see the younger man up close.

The monk cringed in pain from his injuries and tried to sit up. Christophe's firm hand keeping him on the floor convinced him it's best to not move. "That bitch clawed me."

Normally such foul language would offend the abbot and a swift reprimand would ensue afterward. Such was not the case this time, as his mind was elsewhere.

Trying to focus on anything in the dark proved rather difficult for the abbot. "See to it the fire is restarted." Daniela nodded and began doing what she could to get another fire going. "In the meantime, someone get me a torch!"

Jordan, standing in the guesthouse's doorway, quickly ran off to retrieve a torch.

Christophe did what he could to visually examine the amounts of blood soiling Julian's robes and the rest of his body. "I need you to stay awake, Brother. Stay with me." He tried to remove the soaked garment, but Julian writhing in pain and screaming behind clenched teeth stopped him. "We need to get these wounds cleaned before they get worse. Before I can do anything though, I need light!"

Daniela sniffed back a sob. "I'm trying, Abbot. Unfortunately, there are no coals to help start a new fire. The water put them all out!"

The religious figurehead couldn't be mad at the young woman. He could see she was genuinely trying her best to help and felt saddened. There was no telling how bad the monk's injuries were, and he feared the worst. Julian groaned a cry behind hoarse whimpers.

Christophe tried to hold him still by his shoulders. "Try not to move."

Jordan soon returned with a torch in hand and knelt beside the older man. "Does this help?"

"Greatly." The abbot reached for the cross around his neck and extracted the blade within it. His eyes locked onto Julian's panicked ones. All the monk could think about was what this man was about to do. Ideas of being dispatched like other corrupted souls came to mind first. "Whatever you do, don't move." The knife slowly cut down the front of the shredded robes to expose four raw gashes across the younger man's chest. Christophe looked to an empty water bucket lying in front of the fireplace and frowned. "It would be a great help if you could fetch a bucket of fresh, hot water from one of the kitchens."

Daniela could see the only other help in the guesthouse was busy and stood up. "I can do that."

"*No!*" barked the priest. "I'm not letting you out of my sight!" He took the torch and handed it to the woman. "Here, you hold this. You"—looking to Jordan—"get the water."

Once again, the teen scampered off and disappeared outside.

Julian coughed and gripped at his chest in searing, indescribable pain. "I need to burn the body . . . burn the head."

Abbot Christophe shot a quick glance to the decapitated body lying in a thick pool of its own blood in the back corner of the house. Lying close to it was the head, face mangled from being split open. He spoke. "It seems as though it had just fed before being killed."

Daniela tried to not look at the corpse. "How can you tell?"

He studied the gagging woman, a faint and amused smile on his features. "Vampires normally don't have near that much blood in their system unless they have fed. No surprise, given what body count I came across throughout the attack."

Daniela's heart sank hearing the news. How many vampires infiltrated the monastery, and how many monks were killed because? "Exactly how many vampires were there tonight?"

Abbot Christophe answered, "Too many."

*   *   *   *

Jordan didn't stop running his entire trip to the kitchen. Everything was a disorganized disaster all around him. The kitchen was no better. Preparation tables were knocked over, pots and pans littered the floor, as did several cooking utensils. What bothered him the most were several monks huddled around a body. Their heads were hung low in deep sadness, and in getting closer to the body, he found it to be a monk's. Impaled to a fallen table with a large knife in its chest was a muddy, decapitated body of what could be safely assumed as a vampire. No doubt this was the work of Brother Henry.

Kneeling beside the fallen monk was William, eyes squeezed shut. He sobbed. "There was nothing I could do. His wounds were too grievous."

Jordan frowned. "But it's not too late for Brother Julian." William's teary hazel eyes jumped upward to stare at the teen, appalled. "He's been injured and needs medical attention. Abbot Christophe asked me to get some clean water to wash his wounds."

"Where is he? Where's my brother?" William was on his feet with a bucket of fresh water in his hand. The water was just brought in to help him treat the injured monk, but it was too late before it could be used.

"The guesthouse."

Without further hesitation, William charged out of the kitchen.

*   *   *   *

Julian squeezed Daniela's hand and heavily exhaled a strained breath. He wasn't sure if he was trying to remain strong for the abbot or the scared young woman—or even himself, for that matter. By not giving up or showing weakness, he felt he was proving he was stronger than he gave himself credit for.

Christophe gently pressed a strip of linen cloth onto the more severe of the injuries to slow the bleeding. Scattered about him on the floor were other cloth strips he had torn off of a clean bedsheet.

The woman questioned in a shaky voice, "What are we going to do if they come back?"

The thin lips of the older man deeply frowned. "It's not a question of if they come back, but a matter of when."

Julian groaned. "I'd rather not think about that right now."

Pale faced and frenzy eyed, William ran into the guesthouse desperate to see his brother. "Where is he? I heard he was injured!" He glanced over the shoulder of Abbot Christophe kneeling by a bloodied body. *"Julian?"* The young man went to his brother's side as tears swelled up in his eyes. His attention fell on the many stained linen strips draped across four slightly deep cuts. He peeled back one to better examine the wound. Levels of intrigue mixed with panic and relief overcame William's expression. "Did a vampire do this or a cave lion?"

Julian wheezed. "I assure you, it was a vampire."

Abbot Christophe dipped a clean cloth into the half-full bucket of water and began washing the injuries. "With proper tending to, he will be fine."

William choked back a sob of relief and ran his hands over his face, nodding in agreement. "I was fearful his injuries were along those of Gustav's." He heavily sat down on the floor by his brother and trembled all over in extreme relief.

Julian arched a blood-dried brow in mild surprise and weakly smiled. He watched his brother reach for one of the shredded linen cloth pieces lying nearby and dip it in water. The caring touch was gentle when washing away the blood.

Christophe placed the rest of the linen rags beside the monastery physician and strode toward the door. "I trust he'll be in good care. Now if you'll excuse me, I must attend to the rest of the flock. I'm sure some of the younger and more susceptible are in need of spiritual guidance." He gave a smile to the two brothers and felt a rush of emotion steel itself in his chest. Quietly he turned to see Marcos standing beside the door.

The Spaniard was standing as upright as he could, spear ever at his side. "I heard what happened. Will he be okay?"

Christophe nodded and patted him on his hand wrapped around the spear. "Fear not, Brother, for he will live to fight another day. Until then,

I will have another assist you in tending to the girl, till Brother Julian is fully healed."

Marcos nodded in understanding and watched the abbot walk away. He proceeded into the house and frowned at the gut-wrenching scene of the decapitated body. "Why hasn't this been burned yet?" Daniela turned her attention off the two monks in front of her to examine the one behind her. "No worries. I will see to it they are disposed with the other vampires' bodies."

The man knelt down and wrapped his fingers in the corpse's shirt collar with a firm grip. Bone further breaking from being impaled with the spearhead made both Daniela and William grimace in disgust. The body being dragged off smeared a trail of blood behind it in its wake.

Daniela pointed at the trail. "Shouldn't we wash that with holy water? To cleanse the evil, that is . . ."

Julian coughed out, "No point."

William continued for him. "Sunrise is soon on the horizon. Once the sun directly shines down on any spilt vampire blood, it'll burn it away."

18

Flames of Purification

Throughout the course of the night, Valrae stumbled through the woods and over the miles she knew would lead to the abandoned village. Usually the trip to and from the monastery didn't take so long to achieve, but this time, she was injured and unable to travel as fast.

She could see Caliss standing outside the ruins they called refuge and knew why he was waiting. Anger boiled within at his solely waiting for the blood, and she hoped by proving her worth to him, yet again, she would receive higher regard. Valrae urged herself to continue onward, knowing Caliss would be extremely disappointed in her if she admitted defeat to her injuries. She weakly shuffled through the grass and even fell at one point in her closing in on his position. Still, he didn't budge or even flinch to assist her.

His cold, callous eyes narrowed on her falling to his feet. Her bloodied form looked toward the brightening horizon and fluttered upward at him in plea. Surely he wouldn't just leave her there to die in the rising sun?

He snarled in speaking. "Given your lack of returning with your personally chosen team, you were unsuccessful in the job you said you could do." He snorted. "Pity."

She held up a hand streaked red and whimpered. "I kept my word, my lord, and brought you what you wanted."

Caliss completely wrapped a hand around the woman's thin wrist and harshly tugged her to her feet. He deeply breathed in the prominent scent resembling that of a sweet honey to his senses. His mouth encased one of her fingers containing traces of the blood sample and licked away the delightful taste.

His eyes turned bloodshot, and his fanged smile reflected his sinister hunger panging him. Caliss visually examined the woman's once-white flowing gown more closely matching her wild red locks. "So tell me, dear Valrae, what happened?" His voice was degrading and mocking in tone. "You left so confident only to return so broken."

Valrae forced herself to stand upright to show the vampire lord she wasn't broken. "That monk . . ." She hissed in revolt. "The one from the woods with the swords. He's primarily in charge of protecting the blood and is not to be underestimated. He killed my best warrior." Her stance began to falter, and her knees started to give way beneath her in failing strength. She had lost a lot of blood and needed to feed to replenish her energy.

Before she could hit the ground, a pair of strong arms caught her. Caliss collected the woman in his arms and carried her into the safe shadows of the house's depths.

She felt safe and comforted in the strong embrace of her master and lord. All her pains and previous turmoil obtaining what he desired all felt worth it. If it meant being next to the last son of Lilith, as she was now, she'd gladly do it again.

Others who had been anxiously awaiting results of the blood sample saw their master greatly satisfied with what was found. They, too, retreated into hiding as the sun rose over the treetops and onto the ruins of the small settlement.

*　　*　　*　　*

By midmorning, the sun was swallowed by thundering storm clouds. They crawled over the lands and pelted the underlying terrain with freezing rain. Falling water collected on a group of monks, tucked beneath their hoods and gathered behind the monastery cemetery next to the burn pits. Fires blazed high over the decapitated bodies of two monks. Christophe was strict on maintaining procedures over any possible corrupted, even if it meant their own fallen.

At least he had burned them with dignity on a funeral pyre. Earlier in the morning, before the ceremony officially began, the heads were burned separate from the bodies as requested.

The monastery overseer stood on the opposite side of the pit. His gray eyes were heavy with sorrow and matched the darkness of the clouds overhead. In his hands was a tattered leather-bound Bible, which he held open. His voice boomed over the roaring of the fire in reciting passages.

Throughout his reading, closed eyes of many monks squeezed back tears, but not Julian's. His eyes remained focused on the corpses of those he had called family, and his grip around his sheathed swords tightened. Standing on either side of him was Daniela and William. She could see the monk's white knuckles shake with rage. She frowned and gently laid a hand on his, hoping to calm him. He acknowledged her comforting gesture by resting his thumb over her frigid fingers.

It was when the last of the fires of purification died out that most of the monks retreated back into the monastery. Julian wanted to remain with those to bury the ashes, but Christophe insisting he get some rest to heal dissuaded him. It wasn't that he lost interest in honoring the fallen. He just knew resisting the abbot's orders never yielded good results.

Instead, he quietly escorted Daniela back to the guesthouse. There, the fire within the hearth had dwindled to flickering coals.

The monk slid off his water-bogged hood and went to the pile of split logs nearby. "I'll get the fire back going."

Before he could kneel down, Daniela had grabbed his hand, replying, "No, you sit and rest. You're still hurt and shouldn't strain yourself."

The monk met the tear-glazed blue eyes of the woman and smiled. He nodded and, in not wanting to admit she or the abbot was right, wearily sat down at the center table. "How is it I'm supposed to be the one taking care of you and yet you're the one taking care of me?"

Daniela huffed a laugh. "You have been and more than I could ever ask of anyone on my behalf. There's nothing wrong with having someone return the favor."

The two sat in silence until the fire was back burning. From where Julian sat, he could feel the warmth slowly peel away the wet chill on his skin. A trail of water beneath his robes ran down his back, and he jolted upright in the chair.

Julian gave a side gesture of his head in the direction of his room. "Perhaps I should go change into some dry clothes. You should too, before you catch a chill."

The woman rubbed her hands together close to the growing fire. Repulsive spells of smoke and burned bodies managed to get stuck to her clothing, even with it raining. Once the fire was lively on its logs, Daniela quickly changed into clean clothes.

Light knocking sounded on her bedroom door, and she opened it to meet William's distraught gaze. He pressed out a smile for her sake and spoke. "I came by to check on my brother. Seems he's going to try and lie down for a bit."

Daniela returned the monk's smile. "That's good. He needs the rest."

"That he does. Was there anything I could get you before I join Brothers Henry and David in the garden? Abbot Christophe wants everything to be harvested that can be, should the weather get worse."

Slender shrugging shoulders joined an uncertain expression from the woman. "May I join you in working the garden? I could use the distraction of chores right about now."

William nodded. "I see no harm in it. I suggest informing Brother Marcos where you're going to be should he find you absent and become worried."

"Good idea."

19

The Strength Within

Early afternoon slowly dragged on, much like the continuous rainfall. Abbot Christophe watched a rain-drenched and hooded Daniela finish up with her garden work. Her dress was brown with mud on the ends and her shoes not much better. His attention was broken off the gardening woman and to his left to see Julian join him.

He carried his sheathed swords in his right hand, and his left was drawn up into his sleeve for warmth. Closer examination showed the cold didn't seem to faze the monk much. The abbot questioned, "Shouldn't you be resting?"

"I need to practice," came a hasty reply.

Christophe huffed a disbelieving laugh. "Hardly! As I recall, Brother William insisted you get plenty of rest for a quicker recovery. Practicing in the wet and cold is exactly opposite of his instructions."

"You know me, Abbot. I'm not one to sit idle for very long."

William watched the two men from across the vegetable garden field and scowled. He didn't like the smirk his brother was wearing in his conversing with the abbot.

"Do I ever." The older man sighed. "It's a wonder you're able to sit through the daily prayer services!" Both people exchanged glances and smiled to the other. "If you're found practicing with your swords, I will not vouch for you should Brother William voice his objections."

An encouraging sneer from the abbot had Julian on his way to practice beneath a garden perimeter's arcade. William questioned, "What do you think you're doing?" Brothers Henry and David took a moment to stop working and see what was going on.

Julian shrugged and unsheathed his swords. "What does it look like I'm doing?"

Daniela watched the monk further ignore his brother and take a firm stance.

His right foot was behind him, and his left foot in front. Flashes of metal then flew about his form, ending with his right sword held over his head, as though preparing for a downward strike, and his left held close to his side and pointing outward. His movements were fluid in his bringing up his left sword defensively and slashing downward with his right while lunging at the same time. A quick backpedaling of footwork and adjusting his right sword had his blades now crossed before his upper body. His stance was back to its original starting position as his left blade slashed about in front of him and his right held behind his head.

William grumbled. "I thought I told you to take it easy and get some rest!"

Julian resumed his training. "I did get some rest. I spent most of the morning sleeping." He held his swords much the same way he did when starting, except this time, his left sword was held before his upper body. His left sword was held now as it was before. In his right hand slashing downward, he brought his left sword back closer to his body at his side. His right foot stepped forward as he brought his left back behind him. "Can't really get appropriate practice in bed." A roll of his right wrist had his sword along the back of his arm and his left foot swing back out in front. He held his left sword in front of his waist and his right above his head.

Daniela couldn't take her eyes off the man. Brother Henry saw this and leaned over a green bean trellising to quietly state, "It's not polite to stare, my lady."

"He's absolutely beautiful." Her tone of voice was as dreamy as her eyes.

William overheard her and, in his trying to remove a tomato, accidently crushed it in a spurt of shock and anger. His face began to glow red and match his basket of tomatoes draped over an arm.

The green eyes of the young woman continued to watch the dance of footwork and sword swings. Brother David giggled and politely wiggled past William to get to the cabbage bed. Daniela blinked away the dryness settling in her eyes and looked puzzlingly at Henry. "What? Why are you looking at me like that?" Realization overcame her features, and she gasped. "Oh no, no, no, that's not what I meant!" Her pink cheeks and matching nose quickly disappeared behind a blush in embarrassment. "What I meant to say was . . . his practicing." She nodded to herself, but the glint in Henry's eyes stated his being unconvinced. "Yeah, his practicing. The movements in footing and . . ." She brought her gaze to her basket full of green beans and leeks. "I should go take these to the kitchen." Not wanting to subject herself anymore to the mix of stares she had gotten herself in, she quickly fled the garden.

Not wanting to add to the collective gawks on the woman, Julian kept his eyes forward in practicing. His smile, however, couldn't be held back.

*   *   *   *

Julian returned to the guesthouse expecting to find Daniela inside, only to find Abbot Christophe instead. He was kneeling next to the fireplace and stoking the coals. On top of the grate were two fresh logs.

Should he be worried?

The monk anxiously cleared his throat. "Abbot, I wasn't expecting your visit or else I'd have been back sooner."

The older man waved a dismissive hand in the air. "No need to worry about it, dear boy."

Julian sat his sheathed swords on the center table and watched the abbot questioningly. He shot a brief glance toward Daniela's open bedroom door, meaning she wasn't present in the house. "Is something wrong? Did something happen to Miss Daniela?"

"No, no." Abbot Christophe stood up and placed the stoker back on its stand. "I have her and Brother Marcos helping in the kitchen with dinner preparations." Gray eyes settled on hazel ones as the man folded his hands behind his back. "I was once like you . . . young and lost in feelings."

Julian realized where this conversation was going and felt he had William to thank for. "Excuse me?"

A faint smile spread across the abbot's face before continuing. "I wasn't always a devoted of the church, much to the belief of many. I was just like you. I traveled where I could with the money that I had, learning new things along the way. That was when I met Aressa, a beautiful young German woman."

Julian felt uneasy. "Sir, is there a reason for this con—"

The abbot continued. "I had never thought love at first sight was possible, until I met her. We barely knew each other before we got married roughly three months later. She was the absolute love of my life. There was never a bad day when she was around." The faint smile started to fade away into a heartrending frown. "We were married for only two months when she told me she was with child. I had never been more happy in all my life. Me, having my own family and about to be a father." Gray eyes started swimming in tearful eyes.

The older man was silent for a minute, resuming his storytelling in a voice deep with grief. "Aressa wanted to move to Italy. I had told her so much of my birth land that she wanted to see it for herself." He shook his head to himself. "I never should have left Germany."

The monk could see something immeasurable deep in those distant gray eyes. "Did something happen?"

"Not until ten years later when we were told our daughter bore a rare, cursed blood." Christophe paused to deeply sigh and slowly exhaled a labored breath. "The same blood Daniela has. And all I did was introduce her to a danger far worse than I could imagine: vampires. If I wouldn't have brought my daughter from Germany, she would have been safe . . . safe away from *him*!" Christophe took another deep breath in, his lower lip quivering. "That was then that I first met Caliss."

Julian thought about the words being said and on his lessons from the Sect about the blood. His slimmed-down hazel eyes started to widen the more he put the pieces of an imaginary puzzle together. His eyes shot upward to the storytelling abbot, and he felt his blood start to freeze over in breath-stealing horror. Everything made sense now. The details he should've caught before and missed all came flooding over him in remembrance.

The abbot could see the monk's reaction from the corner of his eye, but he didn't falter in his retelling. "He took my little Abigail from me through a powerful hypnosis. It was days before she was found in an alley. She had almost been bled dry. I brought her home to tend to her and even had a physician from the church come to provide aid. For three nights she teetered on the brink of death, suffering from an abnormally high fever. On the third night, the fever finally broke. I woke to find her standing by Aressa's side of the bed. She appeared to be in good health, except . . ." Christophe's gaze lowered, and his tone of voice become further grief stricken. "Something was very wrong."

Julian, pale faced and hand resting on his sheathed swords, spoke in a faint whisper, "Caliss changed her." He dared not take his eyes away from the abbot.

Christophe nodded. "Aye, that he did. I didn't know what to do. I didn't have the heart to kill her seeing how she was my little girl. I feared the worst for my wife, worrying she would end up the same." He brought his gaze back upward and fixated on the fire. "I kept my daughter hidden in the cellar of our house to prevent anyone from finding out. Little did I know Aressa had been turned as well. Apparently, she was secretly feeding

Abigail in small amounts when I was away. The venom took its toll on her after a while. I knew I had to do something for not only was my life in danger, but so were the others in the village. So, I did what I could to protect others around me. I had heard stories from those in the village on how to kill a vampire and did as they had said. I ran a stake through their hearts followed by burning their bodies and scattering their ashes at a nearby crossroads."

Julian felt a twinge of sympathy tug on his insides. Despite what he had just figured out about the older man beside him, he still felt emotionally moved by the story. "I don't think I would have been strong enough to kill those I love. I can't even imagine how it must have felt for you."

Christophe gave a light snort. "I then swore I would do anything I could to find the damned monster and send him back to hell. I hunted him. For years I hunted him and didn't stop till I found him."

Julian tried to get his mouth to form the words to confirm his suspicions. "W-was that when he . . . when he b—"

"Just as he robbed me of my family years prior, he took with him the rest of me the day I confronted him. I then joined the church to seek redemption in what I had done . . . to fight evil with evil. When I told them what I just told you, the Sect allowed me to prove my worth, rather than discard me. They knew I carried a lot of guilt on my shoulders. I felt it my fault that my wife and child were dead."

"Because you moved from Germany back to Italy?"

Christophe nodded once more. "My joining the church has led me to where I am now. The church was aware of the demons lurking in the shadows of the world around us. It's why a separate and secret division within the church was formed. The mission was targeted at eradicating the world of their evil . . . to provide their victims some relief in one way or another."

"I thought the church killed anyone suspected of being corrupted by a vampire's venom."

"They do," the abbot answered, meeting the monk's gaze. "Or should anyway. But there's always that . . . *one* case . . ." Julian huffed a light laugh in understanding what the man meant. "The reason I tell you all this is because I worry for you and Miss Daniela. I can see it in your eyes and how you look at her . . . how she looks at you. Aressa would look at me the same way. It is only natural to care for someone and we cannot choose who we fall in love with. I just hope should something happen to Miss Daniela, you will have the strength to do what is right."

"Like what you did for your wife and daughter . . ."

Christophe nodded. "You will be doing them a favor. Trust me. A life like that, damned to eternal agony, is a purgatory in its own right."

The monk was in disbelief of what he had been requested to do. His grip subconsciously tightened around the handles of his swords. "Abbot, I—"

Christophe interrupted. "I know what I ask is unfair of you and that I ask it of no one else. If you truly care for Miss Daniela, you will do what is necessary *should* something happen."

The abbot turned so that he could face the disconcerted younger man and brought his hands to cup his jaw. Given what he now knew, the chill of those hands should unnerve the monk. Yet somehow they didn't. Instead, he found an odd comfort in those old hands and fatherly eyes.

The older man smiled in his next words. "Never give up on yourself. Let your strength within help you overcome your obstacles." The monk felt torn inside by the abbot's words and sensed there being a meaning to them than just a confidence builder. Julian nodded. "I also ask you not disclose anything I have told you to anyone. Not to William, not to Daniela . . . The only other person within these walls who knows is Brother Henry. Give me your word you will not speak any of it to anyone."

"I give you my word, Abbot."

Christophe nodded. "Good."

20

A Fire within the Cold

Rich aromas of cooking porridge filled the refectorium. The late evening bell chimed dinner, and soon the tables were full of the monastery's occupants eating quietly. Meanwhile, Brother David read the night's lesson.

Afterward, the dirty dishes were collected and cleaned along with the rest of the kitchen. Daniela, Julian, and Jordan stayed behind to help clean the refectorium. Her job was to wipe down the tables as theirs were to sweep the floors.

In light of her embarrassing comment earlier in the garden, Daniela made sure to keep some distance between her and her protector. Every time she'd notice him looking at her, she'd start to blush. Anytime he'd direct his work to be closer to her, she'd go to a different table to wipe down.

This was beginning to bother him. Had Abbot Christophe spoken to her too? Or was she, by chance, afraid he had overheard her comment and was upset by it? Once close enough to the woman to speak and for her to hear, he questioned, "My lady, are you upset with me?"

Daniela sighed and bit her lips together. So many things she wanted to say, to explain herself, but couldn't. "No, Brother Julian, I am not upset with you."

"Then why do your best to avoid me?" He could see her trying to frantically finish cleaning her present table in order to press on to another. "Is it about what you said in the garden, earlier today?"

The woman stopped in her table washing to stare wide-eyed at the inquiring monk. "I do not wish to speak of it and ask you please, let it be." She spun back around and scrubbed fretfully where no dirty spot was.

"Besides, don't you have something you'd rather be doing during evening recreation?"

Julian could see the blush flood past her face and onto her ears. They shined brilliantly against her pinned-up brunette hair. "For what it's worth, I was flattered. Thank you." He leaned against his broom handle and snickered. "Although, the same could be said about you."

Daniela's mind went blank postcomment. She turned around again, but when she went to question him, she saw him walk away. All she could do was frown and leave it as is.

After evening recreation came night prayer, and after that was time to prepare for bed. Marcos went into the guesthouse first and checked every room and every shadow for possible vampire intrusion. Finding nothing, he allowed Daniela to enter.

An iciness had settled throughout the house, and it brought shivers to the woman's spine. No amount of wrapping her cloak around her could ward off the chill. Marcos could see the wood supply was low and rested his spear against a wall next to the fireplace.

"I'll be back with some more wood. Should've done this, this morning but . . ." His voice trailed off in recalling the funeral. "I'll be back in a little bit. Make sure to lock the door behind me."

Daniela analyzed the door hinges and frowned. "Not like it'll do much good."

Marcos jiggled the door and sighed. "Try not to make another mess while I'm gone, okay, Brother?" The Spaniard gave an over-the-shoulder smirk to the other man and went back outside, closing the door behind him.

The young woman smiled and sat down next to the fireplace. She tossed one of the remaining logs onto the grate and stoked the coals underneath. Hopefully the fire would build up soon. She tugged her hair down out the bun she had it tied in and massaged her scalp.

Julian joined her in an attempt to make conversation. "You doing okay? You've been quiet most of the day." The woman nodded. "It's not like you to be so quiet. Did someone say something to you?" Shaking of her head answered his question.

Daniela adjusted in sitting to better face away from the man and angrily prodded the coals. Julian frowned after making the woman more on edge and cautiously got up. Soon afterward, the woman felt his icy hands gather her hair from over her shoulders and slowly comb through the silky brown locks with his fingers.

She then felt his cold touch through the wool fabric of her dress as he began to lightly massage her shoulders. "What are you doing?"

Julian responded, "Trying to get you to relax."

Daniela couldn't deny how good the actions felt against her sore muscles. Being hunched over for the better part of the day in the garden, kitchen, and in helping clean the refectorium made her neck a bit stiff.

The man lightly massaged all of the woman's upper shoulders and lower neck. His fingers gradually snaked to her face and cupped her lower jaw. With the tips of his fingers, he could feel how soft her face was in softly massaging her cheek. Julian could feel the woman relax under his touch and knelt closer to her. A shudder ran down Daniela's spine when she felt the backs of the man's fingers caress down to her neck and across her shoulders.

She turned to face the man and met his soft hazel eyes. They were particularly warming to gaze into in the small firelight's glow. She brought her hands to his face and tenderly caressed it, subconsciously smiling.

Julian took her hands in his and kissed them. He was finding it harder and harder to look away from the woman. He remembered what Abbot Christophe had asked him, and the thought of it burned within his chest. He didn't want to think about ever having to harm her and quickly pushed it from his thoughts. The distance between them closed in a light kiss, and instantly, all worries fell from his consciousness.

The kiss deepened, and they sat there, lost in the other's embrace.

Heavy knocking broke their tender moment. Marcos barged into the house through the door, unintentionally loosening it on his hinges even more. His eyes shifted between the two people. "My apologies, am I interrupting something?"

Daniela realized she and Julian were still sitting suspiciously close to each other and leapt to her feet. "No, Brother Marcos . . . you were not." She ran her hands down the front of her dress and cleared her throat. "Excuse me, Brothers, for it's late and I must get some rest." She gave a curtsy in respect and fled into her room.

Behind her, Julian glared at Marcos. "You're as bad as William when it comes to bad timing. Do you know that?"

Marcos knelt down and unloaded his arm full of wood next to the hearth. "Excuse me?"

"Good night, Brother." Julian reached for his weapon on the table and, too, went to his room for the night.

21

Request

Julian flinched and hissed at the brief, but sharp pain when a bandage was peeled off his chest. "Can you at least be a bit more gentle, Will?" He winced again.

William genuinely tried to be careful. "It would help if you didn't sleep on your stomach. Now the bandages are mashed into the medicinal herbal rub."

"But I sleep better on my stomach!" Another bandage was slowly removed. "Aye," he squeezed his eyes shut. "Geeze, that hurts."

"Such a big baby."

Daniela's bedroom door creaked open, and she groggily emerged. She was wearing his favorite olive drab dress, which he wasn't about to tell her, as he secretly loved how it complimented her eyes. She saw the shirtless, injured Julian being tended to and filled with blush.

Her wide eyes looked at anything else in the room, but the man. "My sincerest apologies, Brothers, as I did not mean to intrude." The woman bit her lower lip in nervousness, not immediately aware she was back to admiring the man's toned physique. Her and Julian's gazes met, and she quickly remembered last night's kiss. "I'm going to go wait in the church for morning adoration." With that, she briskly strode past the two with a hand held up to block her view.

Julian was struggling to maintain a serious composure over his desire to smile. "She's probably squeamish. Even though my cuts are healing, they're still pretty gruesome to—*oowwee!*" He grabbed his chest where his brother had just ripped away the final bandage. "For a physician, you can be a bit thoughtless to those you're tending to."

*   *   *   *

Throughout morning prayer and breakfast, Julian kept reaching for his chest and squirming around. It was obvious he was in some degree of discomfort due to his wounds. Daniela was worried. Throughout the later part of yesterday and into the night, he seemed fine. Perhaps his wounds being tended to this morning had something to do with his flinching around.

Come midday prayer, his fidgeting had become less with the distraction of manual labor. Daniela saw this as an opportunity to ask what had been prying on her mind since the initial vampire attack in the woods. She quietly approached the working monk, helping in collect bundles of hay for transport to the stables, and smiled as innocently as she could.

Her eyes shifted between the man and his weapon resting in the front bench seat of the wagon. "Pardon my interrupting, Brother, but I was curious about something?"

The sweaty man, covered in bits of hay, collected a small rolled up bundle of hay in his arms. He brought it to a blond-haired man, equally hay flecked, and standing in the wagon's bed. Grunting, he hoisted the bundle up to him.

Julian wiped his brow with the back of his sleeve and huffed a deep breath. "What is it you want to know?"

She gave a coy point to his swords. "Could you possibly teach me how to use those things during afternoon recreation?"

The monk's brow lowered and his eyes narrow in question. "Why?"

He was going to say no. She just knew it and hoped she could convince him otherwise. "I want to know how to defend myself if something happens. I'm tired of being helpless while others around me either get injured or . . . *die* for my cause! Please, just show me something. *Anything!*"

The man planted his hands on his hips and studied the woman's pleading eyes for any sign of her joking. "Have you ever used a sword before?" Daniela shook her head.

The second monk spoke from the wagon bed in his stacking the hay bundles. "Have you even spoken to Abbot Christophe about this, yet?" Daniela timidly shook her head and frowned. "Ah."

"It's not easy to learn, Miss Daniela. There is a lot of physical demands and awareness."

"I'm aware of this. I watch you all the time when you practice and train with the others." Daniela quickly caught how her last words must've sounded and closed her eyes, cringing. "I mean, I—"

"I know what you meant," Julian chuckled. Her ivory complexion turned a bright shade of red from blushing, as did her ears. "I will speak with Abbot Christophe after midday prayer, all right?"

Relief in him not saying no swelled within Daniela, but she still felt awkward and embarrassed. "Thank you, Brother Julian." She was hesitant to meet his gaze and quickly jerked it upward to face the second monk. "Brother Luke . . ." A quick curtsey and the woman was rapidly striding away.

*   *   *   *

Daniela nervously dug at her fingernails behind her back. She felt so small in the intense gray eyes of Abbot Christophe, even though not the lone receiver of his unblinking scrutiny. Julian seemed unaffected by the gaze and stood, quietly waiting for an answer.

Christophe at his desk in his personal study and shifted his gaze from one person to the next. Anytime he would look to the young woman, trying her best to hide behind the much broader form of her protector, she would innocently smile.

His gaze fell back on Julian, hands neatly folded over the end of his sheathed weapons held at his feet. "The last thing the Sect wants is her placed in any more danger." The abbot gracefully rose to his feet and approached the two people. "I completely understand your concerns, Miss Daniela, but . . ."

His paused pressed her to question. "But what, Abbot?"

"The Sect fears having you battle trained goes against the point of having you protected."

Daniela's jaw dropped. "What if one my protectors fall? Then what? Twice have I witnessed Brother Julian succumbing to almost defeat within my presence while I did nothing! If I had some type of training I could be more useful!"

Christophe held up a hand to silence the borderline hysterics of the woman. "Trust me, my lady, I know. Which is why I will encourage the training." Daniela's eyes widened and her smile stretch ear to ear.

Julian gave the priest a thanking nod of his head and in being dismissed, escorted Daniela to the training grounds.

22

Tricks of the Trade

Abbot Christophe stood nearby and watched as Julian and Daniela began their first lesson in weapons training. Marcos sat on a stone bench nearby and on one of his knees was his spear. His dark eyes stayed ever attentive on the young woman, desperately trying to remember the defensive moves she was being taught. Julian held up one of his hands with a sword in it and motioned for Daniela to do the same.

William joined Abbot Christophe and questioned in uncertainty. "Do you think this is really a good idea?"

Abbot Christophe never took his gaze away from the two practicing and responded. "It's odd how you and your brother have completely opposite views on things."

The monk's brow twitched in slight question. "With all due respect, Abbot, this is a terrible idea. You're encouraging her to subject herself to further danger! If it is so dangerous for her here to have to subject to fighting tactics, then why not send her away to a major city? Someplace with more people where she can be better protected! The Vatican, perhaps?"

The religious figurehead folded his hands behind him in continuing. "The larger the population, the greater the chance for corruption. At least within smaller walls, there is a better chance to detect and act upon the slightest hint of foul play. Besides, we are one of the strongest monasteries within the Sect."

William grumbled and folded his hands within his sleeves, trudging away to join Marcos on the bench. "Unbelievable."

The Spanish monk scooted over a bit to allow more room for the other man to sit. "He has a point, Brother William. In times like now, one can't be too cautious. Thinking about it, it's best she be prepared for any further sudden situations than not."

"I don't believe this. Am I the only one here who thinks that thing," he pointed a finger at the swords, "Should be rid of?"

"I agree with you," squeaked a man's shy voice. All eyes turned to see Brother Mathew standing behind and shy of where the three people were. "It's our job to protect her. Not her job to protect us."

Christophe glowered at the groundskeeper. "Don't you have work you should be doing?"

Mathew dipped a bow of his head. "Yes, Abbot. I was about to continue them, as a matter of fact. I was only sending out the weekly messages to the villages, asking if any supplies were needed. Our deliveries to the poor are two days away and I wanted an idea of what would be needed." His bashful gaze shifted between the softening abbot's and the other two monks. "That way I could begin preparing what was needed for transport."

Christophe nodded and returned his watch to Julian and Daniela. "Very well. Be on your way, Brother Mathew."

The dismissed man gave another bow of his head and scampered away.

Marcos's dark eyes followed him until eye of sight around the building housing the lavatories. "Always the strange one, he is."

Julian yelled, "Watch out!" just in time for the two monks to see a flash of silver come their away.

Abbot Christophe side stepped out of the flying object's way as William took cover behind the bench. Marcos's training kicked and he reacted accordingly. In a fluid motion, he deflected the sword with his spear and sent it flying off to the side.

Daniela blurted, "Oh hell!" and brought her hands to her mouth in fright.

Christophe called out, "Is everyone all right?"

William peered over the top of the bench seat as Daniela slowly rose from her lying in the cold mud. Everyone exchanged glances with the other and nodded to the abbot. The fear laden eyes of the figurehead rested on the young woman, who cowered at the eye contact.

The man didn't need to say anything for the woman to know what it was he was thinking.

"I am *so* sorry. My hands were cold and it was hard for me to keep my grip. I went to swing my hand out and accidentally threw the sword."

Christophe momentarily analyzed the woman's hands to see her dark pink fingers and sighed. "I believe that is enough training for one day, Miss

Daniela." She nodded in understanding and in regret at her mistake. "Same goes for you, Brother Julian . . ."

The addressed monk nodded his head as well. "Yes, Abbot."

Without saying another word, the abbot turned on a heel and left the training grounds, leaving the four people alone.

William shot his attention to Daniela and questioned in a harsh tone of voice. "What were you trying to do? Skewer me?"

The woman shook her head, stammering. "Of c-course not! I—"

Julian held up a hand to calm his brother. "It's an easy mistake, Brother. She meant no harm, I'm sure."

"*No harm?*" William snorted. "What if Brother Marcos hadn't been there, hmm? I could have had a sword ran through my chest if not be decapitated!"

Marcos stood before the ranting monk and patted him on the shoulder. "Enough, Brother. Forgive and forget, shall we?" He urged the other man to join him. "Come, let us get ready for midafternoon prayers."

William heavily sighed and shook his head, following his fellow brethren and friend. Julian retrieved his other sword lying in the grass some feet away and sheathed them together. "Not to worry, my lady. We all make mistakes. No one is perfect, even those who have the mentality that think they are." He caressed her face and brought a hand to uplift her chin. He gazed deeply into her green eyes and comfortingly smiled. "I will speak with him, later."

Daniela weakly nodded.

*　　*　　*　　*

Caliss sat beside on the floor and beside a wrought iron stand containing several, half melted candles. Sitting on an upward bent knee was a gray and white courier pigeon and in his hand was a piece of parchment. His blue eyes took in every detail the message had to offer.

Coming into the house and lower faced covered in blood was Valrae. She licked at her equally bloody fingers and smacked her lips. "What do you have there, my love?"

She joined him and knelt down to look at the parchment, herself. Caliss quietly laughed to himself. "It appears the girl is trying to learn sword skills from her protector." He tossed the message aside with complete disregard to Valrae trying to read it. "Looks like I had better make my move and soon."

"Allow me to accompany you."

"No." Caliss took the pigeon in his hand and stood up. "I will be going alone, on this one." He met Valrae's worrisome face. "Not to worry though, my dear. I have a plan and if that little weasel of an informant knows what's best for him, he'll keep his vow to me."

23

A Brother's Loyalty

The entire time during midafternoon prayers, William gave no acknowledgment to Daniela or his brother. Instead, he kept his eyes forward and stayed to himself. This greatly bothered Julian and he was going to make sure he set things straight with the other man.

After prayers were over, Daniela accompanied Marcos in tending to livestock. Julian caught up with William in the vegetable gardens during their work hours. Older brother glared at younger. "How much longer are you going to continue letting your arrogance control you?"

William threw his hand trowel into the soft dirt and leapt to his feet to return the confrontational attitude. "Funny you should ask that. How much longer are you going to continue letting your ignorance control you?"

"I don't understand why you're so passively hostile to Miss Daniela."

William laughed in disbelief. "You're really going to ask me that?" His false smile shifted to a sterner, concrete glare. "Ever since you first saw her, you have completely disregarded your vows as a follower of God." He took a step closer to the older man. "You are not the changed man you told the church and myself you were. No. When I first saw you after all those years, I had hopes we could be a family, again." He shook his head. "Was I ever wrong. My *real* brother left when I was eight and hasn't been back since. The man who calls himself my brother is nothing more than a memory of my past. You talk about my arrogance? Try looking at yourself in a mirror, for once." Julian stood there in complete awe to the verbal lashing he was receiving. "You have no right being within these walls and calling yourself a Brother to those who are wholly devoted to the church and to God. Your morals are loose as are your eyes and lips for empty promises and vows. As long as you continue to run about, following Miss Daniela out of lust, you will never be my brother in blood or in faith."

Julian choked out a gasp. He opened his mouth to say something, but couldn't. His hazel eyes pooled with tears, and his heart crumbled in his chest. "Is that how you feel?" William didn't answer. He only picked up his trowel and continued working. "You have no idea how I really feel about her, do you? Or you, for that matter. Every thought that maybe the reason I'm 'following Miss Daniela out of lust' is because I genuinely care for her? I came to appreciate a person's company and worth when several years back in Japan. Remember that family I told you about? The old man and his daughter? He cared for me like I was his own son. Something our father never did for me. He was too wound up over you being the second coming to the family."

William scoffed. "Perhaps if you had more dignity and respect for others around you . . ."

Julian knelt down to be better on level with the other man. "Watching someone I more saw as a father than my own taught me a lesson in his death. Sometimes the greatest things around us are that which we take for granted. Disregard me as your brother all you want, but it won't change the fact you're mine. I forgive you for your flaws and transgressions every day. If you're going to sit there and judge me for mine, then perhaps I'm not the one who shouldn't be within these walls . . ."

William stopped in his working as soon as the words and meaning to them sunk in. Before he could say a thing, he was alone and the other man gone.

*   *   *   *

Daniela watched Brother Henry with mesmerized eyes. He was chopping an onion and proficiently at that. His quick hands and quicker chopping knife never faltered from one onion to the next. When a stack of two or three would start to take over his chopping board, he would scrape them off into a large wooden bowl and continue.

She smiled. "Amazing, Brother."

Henry thought nothing about it and was momentarily thrown off by her comment. "Pardon me?"

The woman gestured to his motions with her eyes. "It never ceases to amaze me at how fast you are in preparing the vegetables."

"Oh," the heavyset man cheerful giggled and reached for another onion to chop. "All in good practice, my lady."

William entered the kitchen and with a few ripe tomatoes in hand. "Managed to harvest these before the birds could get to them."

He stood next to an empty food prepping table and sighed. He watched Daniela and Henry laugh and talk and frowned. The words Julian had said to him in the garden burned in his mind and pained his heart. He wasn't sure how long he stood there, blindly staring at the tomatoes on the table.

Henry snapping his fingers inches from his face jerked back to reality. "Brother? Is something wrong?"

William forced a smile and shook his head. "No, of course not." The other man gave him a strange sideways glare when going back to preparing his vegetables. "Miss Daniela," he politely questioned. Her heartwarming smile was sincere. How could she be so kind hearted to him after how he spoke to her, earlier? "Would you please help me in washing and preparing the tomatoes?"

The woman gave a nod and joined the man.

They were almost done when Julian and Marcos entered the kitchen. The Spaniard had his spear with him and a light cut beneath his left eye. Henry saw it and raised a brow. "I thought, by now, you would know how to properly play with sharp toys." He gave a swift chop of a potato with one of his knives, smiling mischievously.

Marcos scoffed. "I do. It's just when the other person," he gestured to Julian, "Gets a little over zealous when playing with his."

The discussed monk shrugged. "I think Abbot Christophe is right . . . you're getting too slow. You should work on that, more." He tried to wiggle a finger underneath Daniela's hand to sneak a piece of chopped tomato, but a smack of her hand on his stopped him.

"Do not spoil your dinner." Her sharp green eyes silently scolded him. "You can wait like everyone else. Unless, of course, you're the evening's lector . . . which I know you're not." She nudged him away and started chopping up a second tomato.

The whole time, William watched the two people's interactions. In doing so, noticed Julian refusing to acknowledge him if even visually. William nudged a piece of chopped onion toward the other man. Daniela cocked her head to the side in annoyance and planted a hand on her hip.

Julian took the offer as a type of peace offering and accepted it. His hand snatched it up before Daniela's could take it away. He happily chewed on the juicy morsel, smiling. William spoke. "I doubt one small piece of tomato is going to spoil his dinner. Not when he can put the pigs to shame in how much he can consume. My dear brother is the reason settlements outside the monastery walls are starving."

Daniela snickered, Julian smirking. "I'm not sure if I should be complimented or offended . . . *Brother* . . ."

William scraped his chopped tomato into a small bowl. "With you, they're one and the same. Now, if you'll excuse us, we need to finish preparations for dinner." He dumped the tomato in with the chopped onion and growing stack of potatoes. "Unless, of course, you're here to help?"

*   *   *   *

Brother Mathew finished his sweeping out the courier pigeon cage when a rustling of feathers got his attention. He brought his attention to the source and saw a gray and white pigeon fly into the cage and keenly watch him. Tied to one of its tiny legs was a tattered piece of parchment. The monk almost stumbled over himself and his broom to get to the bird.

His fingers untied the string around the message and read the note to himself. His entire posture sank, but he knew what was being asked. He stuffed the note into his robes and turned to leave the cage, almost colliding into Abbot Christophe.

The monk fell motionless. Those gray eyes appeared as though reading his everything thought. "Abbot Christophe. You startled me! I never even heard you walk up!"

The much older man studied the other younger man's frantic brown eyes. "Not to worry, my son. Is something wrong? You seem a bit alarmed."

Mathew ardently shook his head. "No, sir. I was just afraid you were a vampire, is all. It's getting dark outside and well . . . you just scared me." He wiped his sweat forming palms onto his robe in anxiousness.

Christophe patted the man on the shoulder. "I see one of the pigeons returned from your sending them out, earlier. I trust it came back with a reply?"

"Yes, yes, it did." He could feel heat start to rise beneath his robe's collar and fill his face with nervous blush. Not to worry though, Abbot. I will take care of everything in time for the village supply runs."

The abbot could see something was wrong. The shifting in his eyes to his fidgeting with his robes. Everything about his demeanor bothered him. Then again, this particular young man was always socially awkward. A simple visitation from one of London's Bishops had him falling over himself in stress.

Christophe nodded and gave a gentle squeeze to the groundskeeper's shoulder. "Come. Dinner is ready."

The much younger man bowed a nod and followed, glancing back over his shoulder to the gray and white pigeon.

24

Messages from the Inside

Caliss watched the sunset give way to the night. His icy blue eyes stared off into the distance where the monastery lay. Light from a full moon washed the settlement ruins through the passing over clouds. Calling from a pigeon sounded from somewhere in the darkness of the abandoned settlement, the vampire lord looking to the source. The bird paced about the railing of the house he had taken refuge in and strode over to it.

He gently collected the bird in his hand and slid the note off its leg. Unrolling it revealed confirmation of his plans falling underway. Figures slipping out of the shadows captured his peripheral vision and he quietly laughed to himself. With his hand cradling the pigeon, he crushed it and tossed the lifeless body aside.

Starving vampires fought over themselves to take the pigeon's body for themselves, Caliss paying them no attention. Tucked away in her own shadow's concealment was Valrae. Her eyes watched the man discard the note to the ground and leave the ruins via its main road.

*　　*　　*　　*

Night prayer ended and the monastery begin its late night routine. Those who were not on perimeter patrol went back to the dormitory to prepare for bed. Marcos went to the perimeter wall as Julian escorted Daniela to the guesthouse.

Abbot Christophe calling for the two people stopped them feet from the guesthouse. "Brother Julian, might I ask of your assistance with a task?"

The monk looked to the young woman beside him. She smiled in reassurance. "I'll be fine. Brother Marcos is nearby should I need assistance."

Accepting the answer as it was, Julian followed Christophe back to his private study. The abbot called to the patrolling monk. "Brother Marcos, please keep a watch on the guesthouse. Brother Julian will be accompanying me for a short time."

The patrolling monk gave an obliging nod of his head and returned his watch to lands stretching out beyond the outside wall.

Daniela went to the guesthouse and threw her entire body weight into the door. Much to her relief, it opened, and she was allowed to enter the chill within. She wasn't surprised to find the fire had died, and she sighed.

*   *   *   *

Mathew hurried down the stairs leaving the wardrobe with his arms full of brown woolen robes. He rounded a corner leading outside and saw Henry leaving the kitchen, carrying buckets of food left over from dinner.

The plump and cheerful monk gave a nod to the other. "Working a little late, are you not Brother Mathew?"

The awkward monk smiled behind his arm full of robes. "Merely gathering the dirty robes and linens to be washed in the morning."

"Need any assistance? These are my last buckets to take to the pig troths." Henry gave a gesture to the buckets of slop. "I can help you, if you'd like."

Red hair of the monk tossed about in a head shake. "No, no, Brother. I can manage." His brown eyes shifted to the full moon overhead and felt the weight of time close in pressing upon him. "I should hurry up and finish my chores. Abbot Christophe doesn't like anyone not doing patrols to be out past dark."

Not wanting to wait around for further questions, Mathew loped off. He gave a glance over his shoulder to the other monk in hopes he wouldn't follow. Last thing he wanted was to be caught in a suspicious act. He could see Brother Luke on the perimeter wall and quickly loped to the wash house.

The patrolling monk paused in his strides to look around. He was happy for the moonlight as it allowed to see what he otherwise wouldn't without it. He could see Mathew run into the washhouse and cocked a smile. Seems the oddball of the monastery was always busy with some kind of work when not resting, in prayer or attending meals. When Luke turned back around, his body froze where he stood.

His eyes met the bloodshot eyes of a snarling vampire. He opened his mouth to yell out, but the attacking vampire stopped him.

Caliss constricted his already paralyzing grasp around the monk's throat and crushed it. With a twist of his wrist, the monk's neck was broken. The vampire jumped from atop the perimeter wall, dragging his fresh kill behind him and went for the wash house.

Mathew yelped at the front door being busted open and Caliss enter. The frightened man pressed his body into a stone wall of the building and whimpered. "Master . . . please . . . I've done as you've asked. Have mercy on me." The vampire bared fangs and lunged for the horrified monk.

*   *   *   *

Marcos sighed and cast his attention to the guesthouse. All was quiet. He could see a hooded monk casually stride past and thought for a moment, it was Julian. The figure carried no swords, so it couldn't be him. He called to the figure. "Brother . . . what brings you to roam about so late?"

The man stopped in his walked to answer. "I was on my way to the tower to take watch."

Marcos nodded. "Very well. Proceed," and he watched the monk disappear into the shadows. Feeling he had already taken enough attention off the outside of the walls, he returned to his patrols.

Inside the guesthouse, Daniela smiled in content to the roaring fire and got up, retrieving a candle off the center table. She carried it to her room to help her find a book to read. Might as well enjoy the peace and quiet and try to read a little bit before bed. She heard the house's door be opened and figured it to be Julian returning from assisting Abbot Christophe.

After finding her desired book, she returned to the living area of the house. Julian was nowhere to be seen and shrugged. He was probably in his room preparing for bed. Still wearing a smile, the woman reclaimed her spot beside the fireplace to read. She got comfortable and thumbed through the pages to one she had folded down at the corner.

In her reading, she kept feeling an icy waft of air tickle her neck. At first the thought Julian hadn't closed the door all the way and glanced over her shoulder toward it. Much to her curiosity, she found the door closed. Perhaps, the source of the draft was from the gap between the door's base and stone floor. Or maybe the hinges had loosened, even more, and a draft coming from there. Pushing out of her mind, she continued reading.

But something still didn't feel right. She felt the chill again and this time different than before. This felt more like someone was breathing on her neck. The hairs on the back of her neck and on her arms stood on end in recognizing she wasn't alone.

Out of paranoia, she looked back to where her protector's room was. "Brother Julian? Are you there?" No answer. The bedroom door opened and a brown woolen robed figure emerge. Daniela exhaled a labored breath in relief. "Brother Julian . . . you had me scared for a moment." She closed her eyes and laughed to herself. "For a moment I thought you were a . . . no, never mind. It's nothing." She waved a hand in the air.

A haunting and unfamiliar voice finished her sentence. "A what?" The hood was drawn back to fully expose Caliss's head. "A vampire?" His last words were a subtle growl. He shed the robe and tossed to the floor in disgust.

Daniela's breath started to labor and her heart ardently beat in her chest. There was a part of her telling her to not turn around, but she did anyway. Her green eyes trailed across the floor and up to the new form. The mysterious man flexed the fingers of his right hand as Daniela's body went motionless. She whimpered in terror for help, but her voice wouldn't fully form. It was as though an invisible force had her by the neck, restraining her.

Caliss approached the woman, her better able to see him. His bare feet were caked in mud mixed with what looked like speckles of blood. Red speckles matching a series of along his right arm's sleeve stood out in contrast to the gray linen fabric. His long blond hair curtained his pale, emaciated face where haunting ice blue set in bloodshot eyes stared back.

His eyes reflected the light from the flickering flames and sneered spitefully. In raising his hand, the woman stood under his control.

Daniela, under an apparent hypnosis of the mysterious stranger, moved in closer to him. The woman's spacey eyed gaze lazily drifted upward to meet her puppeteer's. He deeply breathed in the woman's scent and became lost in her natural sweet honey scent.

His elongated fangs became visible when he spoke. "I've been waiting for you." He neared closer to her neck and licked at the warm, sweet skin. "You're more desirable then I expected." His cold hand caressing her cheek prickled the hairs of her skin. "I will make you mine and there is nothing your damned church can do to stop me."

The young woman whispered, "Caliss," in a voice she didn't recognize as her own. She had no control over her body, anymore, and was now at the mercy of this creature.

Daniela brought a hand around the back of his neck and pulled him closer to her. He obliged and brought his other hand around her waist. She could feel his lips caress over the vulnerable vein pulsing with each beat of her heart and just knew this was her end. Her mind screamed for her to run, but her body wouldn't follow through no matter how hard she tried.

The moment was interrupted, however, when the iron handle of the room's wooden door jiggled. Creaking of the hinges following afterward gave way to Julian entering the room.

25

Blood and Shadows

Julian froze in place as soon as he saw the dazed Daniela standing motionless and unresponsive. He recognized her actions as being symptoms to a vampire's hypnosis. Whoever did this couldn't be too far away. Why weren't the bells rang in warning of an intruder?

He rushed to her side and frantically patted her on the face to revive her from the trance. "Daniela? Daniela, wake up. It's all right." The young woman swayed in her stance and her eyes flutter closed in her collapsing. Julian quickly acted and caught her. He lowered her to the floor and began searching her neck for any bite marks.

Much to his great relief, she was uninjured. "Abbot Christophe will want to know about this." The monk collected the young woman in his arms and was about to leave when he turned to face Daniela's attacker blocking his way to the door. "Caliss," spat Julian. "You will not harm this child of God."

Caliss let out a nerve-racking laugh. "Weak mortal and your God."

Julian hastily laid the unconscious Daniela back on the floor and whilst never tanking his eyes away from the slowly approaching vampire. "You won't get to her that easily." The monk then removed his sheathed swords from his rope belt. He was prepared to do whatever was necessary to protect the young woman.

Caliss laughed, again, in mockery. "Do you honestly think that is going to stop me?" The vampire hissed. "Pathetic."

"I swore to the Sect, to Abbot Christophe and most of all, God, that I would let *nothing* happen to her." He lowered his brow and cut his eyes down on the threatening figure. "And I'm one to keep my word till death."

Caliss gave a cocked nod of his head to the opposite man's last words. "Then to your death, mortal!"

In the radiance of the fire's glow, the two men began to fight. Julian jerked his swords' handles to extract his blades from the other, but Caliss was quicker and stronger to counter him. In a matter of moments, the vampire blocked the monk's dominate hand unsheathing the sword using his left arm. He then landed a punch along the right side of the other's face with his right fist to daze him. Using his left hand, Caliss reached under Julian's arm to grab the back of his shoulder and pull him downward. A sharp blow to the back of the head using his right elbow sent the monk hunching forward where a knee met his face.

Julian's grip on his swords faltered as they fell to the floor and rolled off to the side.

"This is what Christophe has protecting the blood?" The vampire reached down and hurled the monk to the other side of the room, where he crashed with the stone wall. "Your efforts are in vain, monk. I'm going to make you watch the girl become my queen while you slowly die." Caliss strode over to his hapless, groaning victim and pinned him against the wall he had just been thrown against.

Julian wearily lifted his bloodied face to meet his attacker's gaze and scoffed. "Here I was thinking you would be a real threat. Guess not." When he had been lying on the floor, he took the open opportunity to retrieve a knife concealed within the sleeve of his robe.

The attacker bared fangs and closed the distance between them to bite his newly obtained prey. He stopped shy of burying his fangs in the other man's neck to let out a sharp growl in pain.

Julian had and stabbed the other man in the chest.

The man fell to the floor in a daze from the vampire's grip on him loosening and noticed his twin swords lying on the floor nearby.

Caliss wrenched the knife from his bloody chest and watched the monk stumble over to retrieve his prized weapon. The vampire licked the soaked blade of the knife and thoughtlessly pitched it off to the side

The vampire growled in amusement to the monk taking a defensive stance with weapon in hand. "You honestly think your little stick can do anything more to me that your paper cutter couldn't?"

Caliss charged at him again, Julian narrowly avoiding getting hit by dropping to his knees and bending backward.

The monk used one of his swords to slash across the vampire's chest and leapt back up to his feet. Caliss stumbled forward, a bit, hand clutching the gash at his chest. Julian adjusted his grip on his swords to give him max length's reach on his opponent and stood at the ready for another attack.

Caliss snorted and lunged at the monk, again. Once more, the vampire was weaving and dodging the attacks. He held up an arm and deflected a sword slash by grabbing the man's wrist and seizing it.

A sharp pain ran through left side of Julian's face as the vampire backhanded him. In a quick flash of movement, Julian pierced the abdomen of the vampire.

Caliss grabbed at the monk's neck with one hand and in using the other, extracted the blade from his gut. The young man tried to strike the looming attacker with his other sword, but was unable to move. "This . . . ends . . . now, monk," growled Caliss, baring fangs.

A paralyzing pain streaked through the monk's body as his mind tried to grasp what had happened. He had failed. He could feel the vampire further bury his fangs into the tender flesh of his neck. Warmth from his blood started to stream down his chest and back. He tried to cry out but found himself incapable as the muscles in his throat seized up, cutting off his words. An unfathomable burn coursed through his veins, making his arms and legs go numb and vision blur. Every time he tried to move, he found the burning sensation multiplied. Still, the feasting vampire showed no remorse.

The strength of the monk was starting to give out as his legs buckled beneath him. Slowly, the vampire lowered the dying man to the floor without breaking away from the bite.

Memories washed over the incapacitated monk, stemming back from his childhood days, through his days adventuring, time spent in Japan to finally present day.

The vampire could feel the weak man beneath him squirm. He savored the agony his prey was enduring. He broke the bite long enough to meet the weary man's half lidded eyes. Caliss curled up upper lip in a lurid sneer. "Till death, right, monk? Isn't that what you said? Tell me, is it worth it? Is *she* worth it?"

Julian hoarsely choked out, "Go back to hell."

Caliss laughed and was about to resume his biting when a pain shot through his upper back. He reached for the source and was able to catch a glimpse of the now conscious Daniela standing behind him. The vampire roared out in pain and jerked the cross concealed knife from his back. The silver of the metal and holiness of the symbol burned into the palm of his hand.

Daniela made a run to the door, yelling as loud as she could. "Vampire! Marcos, help! Vampire!"

The vampire discarded his current victim and lunged for the young woman. Any further words were cut off by Caliss grabbing her hair, spinning her around and backslapping her to the floor.

Marcos barged into the guesthouse, spear at the ready and eyes quickly falling on the attacker. Keeping a firm grip on the bottom of his spear, he thrust it forward and nicked the vampire between the bottom of the neck and top of the shoulder. Caliss howled in pain. The monk made another attack, Caliss stopping him. He deflected the spear and grabbed it by the shaft.

A powerful swing sent the second monk across the center table and crashing to the floor.

Knowing more reinforcements were soon to come, Caliss stumbled outside and to his escape.

Daniela propped herself upright and looked the unconscious, blood soaked Julian. He was sprawled out on the floor and not moving. Was he even breathing? Her heart caught in her chest and she choked out a sob. She crawled across the floor and to the dying man. "No, no, no, no, no," she cried. She remembered what Abbot Christophe did when tending to his cuts across his chest and applied what pressure she could to the bite mark at his neck. Her sobs continued. "Please, please, please."

Marcos used his spear to stabilize him in getting back to his feet. He glanced around the guesthouse to see the vampire was gone. Hearing the woman's sobbing, he brought his attention to the source.

Daniela yelled to him, "Go get help!"

Marcos wanted to. He genuinely wanted to fetch help, but couldn't. The Spaniard shook his head regretfully. "I'm sorry, my lady I . . . I can't leave you unattended."

Tears freely fell from the woman's eyes. "Damn it, he's dying!"

Marcos felt his own eyes water with tears and exhaled a labored breath. "I'm sorry . . ." he wheezed in restrained cries.

Outside, the bells of the monastery rang out in echo. Daniela held the injured and barely responsive man to her chest and cried the hardest she ever had in all her life. "Please, don't die. Please . . ."

Even with her hand pressed firmly against his neck, she still felt his life slip between her fingers and onto her dress.

26

The Damnation

William entered the guesthouse with eyes scanning the interior. They instantly fell on the frantic Daniela holding the bloody and almost unrecognizable Julian in her lap. Gut wrenching sickness overcame him and he held a hand to his mouth. Not because of the sight of so much blood, but because of his deathly looking brother.

The young woman's crying out brought him back to reality. "Brother William, please do something! He's been bit and is dying!"

William fell to his knees at his brother's side and for a moment, completely forgot all training he had received from the Sect. "Brother!"

"Do something!" screamed Daniela.

A quick examination led to the grim discovery of the gash-like bite on the left side of the man's neck. Unfortunately, the injury was still freely bleeding. The monastery physician covered his hand with his robe's sleeve and replaced Daniela's hand with his own. He hoped it would better stop the bleeding.

William sobbed, "Go get Abbot Christophe! Go—now!"

Daniela shoved past Marcos in her running out of the guesthouse. The Spaniard followed. "Wait! You can't just run off!" He pursued her.

The woman snipped back, "I don't see you doing anything to help save him!"

She ran toward Abbot Christophe's house, the outside of the monastery filling with curious monks. Some were armed, others not. They stood aside upon seeing the frantic young woman ran past them, calling for Christophe.

She arrived to the abbot's house and frantically pounded on the door in desperation. "Abbot Christophe! Please, you must come help! Abbot Christophe!"

Her relentless assaulting the door continued, an answer behind her stopping her. Gray eyes deep with panic studied the blood soiled young woman. "Good heavens, child, what is it?"

Daniela spoke between frenzied breaths and sobs. "We must hurry! Brother Julian has been bitten by a vampire! I think . . ." she tried to swallow to moisten her dry mouth. "I think it was Caliss."

Almost as though she had said herself, Christophe grabbed the young woman and began analyzing her neck and arms. "Were *you* bitten?"

The woman shook her head and took the man's icy hands in her shaking ones. "Come on, we don't have much time!"

Christophe pulled out of the woman's grasp to retreat back into his chambers. "I must get some things that could possibly save the boy." Bustling around could be heard from behind the partially ajar door. Soon he exited the shadows of the house with a worn, leather bag in his hands. "Let's go." The two trotted to the guesthouse, Christophe appearing as though running into an invisible wall. He stopped dead in his tracks and looked to Daniela in panic. "Quickly, invite me inside."

She couldn't believe he was doing this again. Why? She was dressed. There was no privacy being invaded. "Yes, come inside . . . something, whatever . . . just help Julian!"

The abbot entered the house and followed the trail of blood drops to the panic-stricken William. In his arms was his bloody and motionless brother. The monk stated in a voice full of urgency. "I've been trying to slow the bleeding the best I can, Abbot, but nothing seems to work!"

Christophe dropped the leather bag down onto the floor with a thud and knelt beside the seemingly lifeless man. The abbot began to feel of Julian's neck, sighing a relief. "He's alive, but barely. We must hurry though, as we don't have much time." The man harshly tugged his bag open to rummage through the contents. He grumbled in irritation at the miscellaneous disheveled reagents. "Ah hah!" He held up a fist sized vial containing a clear liquid. "Holy water from Jerusalem. Nothing quite like it."

Graciously, the abbot stood up and rushed over to the fireplace, removing the cork from the vial to access the blessed liquid within. He withdrew the cross concealed knife from beneath his black robes and murmured in a breathless whisper.

Her focusing on the older man was brought to Brother Henry entering the guesthouse. He gasped at the sight of William and Julian and joined the woman's side to watch the abbot.

Daniela able to make out it being Latin. The young woman intently watched Christophe's actions, behind a wrinkled brow, as he sprinkled a few drops of the Jerusalem holy water onto the knife blade. Satisfied the knife was inundated enough, he placed the tip of the blade into the fireplace just far enough to become imbued in flame. The water on the blade simmered in the heat as the dagger tip began to glow a dull orange.

Christophe hastily got to his feet and returned to the aid of Julian. He removed William's hand from the bite wound and continued his Latin chanting while firmly pressing the blade onto the blood oozing wound. The smell of burnt flesh arose from the smoke of the simmering flesh, Daniela choking back a sob at the sight. He held it there for as long as necessary, repeating his chanting.

Julian hoarsely moaned and his back arch against the searing pain tearing through the already painful gash at his neck. Desperately, he reached for the source of the pain only to be restrained by William's tight grasp. Henry and Daniela held onto the other's arm and hands in fear.

Abbot Christophe held the blood caked knife out for someone to take. Henry broke away from Daniela's clutches to take it. The older man continued. "That should stop the bleeding. A vampire's venom thins the blood, allowing it to flow more freely and not clot up. Makes feeding easier. Once there is enough venom in the blood, clotting becomes impossible. If not tended to almost immediately after the bite is broken, the victim will die of blood loss. Should there be any left after feeding, that is."

William took a clean part of his robe's sleeve and wiped away a layer of sweat that was beginning to form on his brother's brow. "He will be all right, won't he?"

Christophe was back shifting through the contents of his leather bag and replied. "If you mean, will he change? There's always the remote possibility."

William cradled his brother closer to him in fear of the abbot's words. "What are the chances of that happening?"

"It depends on how much of the venom the body absorbed." Christophe paused in his shuffling through is bag to study the eerily pale and sweat enveloped Julian. The older man pressed his lips into a grim expression and sighed. Seeing the desperation of a brother's love in William's eyes, Christophe replied. "In all the years of serving the Sect, only a select few victims were saved from changing."

"You're not going to kill him . . . are you? I know per the Sect's orders, anyone bitten or suspected of being corrupted by a vampire is to be put to death." William shook his head and protectively shielded his older brother the best he could.

Christophe would rather not answer the question and avoided answering. His eyes slimmed down where Daniela stood, nervously gnawing on her fingernails. "Did you happen to see what the vampire looked like? You said you thought this work of Caliss."

She nodded her head in response, never taking her gaze away from the dreadfully pale monk on the floor. "Y-yes I did."

Christophe stared at her in anticipation and raised a brow in impatience. "Well? Spit it out, girl!"

"He was tall." She held up her hand above her head where she roughly guessed her attacker's height to be. "Slightly taller than me with long blond hair and—"

"Caliss." Christophe and Henry said simultaneously.

The young woman's face contorted into bewilderment. "So it was him, then."

Christophe removed another vial from his bag and uncorked it. "I'm sure you've already heard the stories of his origins and the level of his power?"

He could see Daniela nod from the corner of his eye while continuing in his tending to Julian. The vial was brought to the barely parted lips of the ill man for him to drink.

The woman held a hand to her neck, realizing the level of danger she was just in. "Why did he hesitate in biting me? I . . . I don't remember what stopped him. Everything is a blur. I know it has something to do with Brother Julian stopping him." Marcos shot his squared down, dark eyes on the woman. Daniela bit her lips together. "Brother Marcos helped too."

Abbot Christophe watched the injured man weakly cough at the bitter liquid slowly being poured into his mouth. William continued to cradle his brother and brought his rage forged gaze to Daniela. "Where the hell were you during this time? What about all those lessons my brother taught you?"

Christophe interrupted in a restrained tone of voice. "Brother William, that will be enough!"

The younger man didn't listen. "Julian almost died because of you!" His tear pooled eyes snapped back over to the abbot. "I want to know where she was during this whole thing!" He returned his yelling to the recoiling woman. "Why didn't you do something?"

The girl tried to recall what happened and shook her head. "I remember coming back here and starting a fire. It had gone out during evening recreation and night prayer. Afterward, I thought I would read for a little bit. That's when I heard the guess house door open. I thought it was Brother Julian returning form helping Abbot Christophe. When I looked around, I saw no one. It wasn't long after that Caliss came out of Julian's room. That's the last thing I remember. I don't know what happened after that, but I came to, Julian was on the floor with that monster . . ." the woman fought back threatening sobs. "Biting him!"

"You should have killed Caliss when you had the chance." The angst distorted features of William reflected everything he felt inside

A gurgling sound from Julian's throat quickly broke the ensuing verbal fighting, Christophe quickly acting in response. "Roll him over on his side. If not he'll asphyxiate." The two men carefully did so as the monk vomited the water he just drank onto the floor. The abbot's already stress worn face melted into a more deeply disturbed frown.

Henry studied the emotionally stressed priest. "Oh no . . ."

Christophe shoved the cork back into the bottle and hatefully slammed it back into the bag. "I was hoping to cleanse his body of the venom before it began to set in."

The abbot analyzed the glazed over hazel eyes of the monk. William was horrified. "I thought you said he wouldn't turn!"

Christophe shook his head and rested a hand on the feverish forehead of the monk in a hot-cold sweat. "The venom pulsing through the remaining blood in his veins is beginning to prepare his body for the change continuation." Daniela admitted defeat to her emotions and began to hysterically cry. "Caliss will return in due time to finish the transformation. We must keep a diligent eye out for anything suspicious until Brother Julian completely heals."

William wiped away the access sickness from his brother's mouth and watched hopelessly at the slightly older man that had been for him nearly all of his life. "So this is temporary, then?"

Abbot Christophe solemnly collected the removed items from his leather bag and replied. "It's too early to say for sure."

The younger monk's heart visibly sank further in his eyes.

"I have seen victims of vampires react to the venom differently. For some, it gradually changes them over a few hours to days. Others, it kills instantly or slowly, overtime."

William's eyes widened with a thought and glanced over to Daniela on the bed. "What about her? She can cure him!"

Christophe studied the young woman to see her appearing somewhat hopeful. As much as he favored the idea of saving the ill monk, he shook his head. "He isn't a vampire. Just because the poison runs through his veins, her blood can't change it." The abbot moved his leather bag aside. "Brother William . . . Brother Henry, help me get him out of these bloody clothes. Brother Marcos, please get me some clean robes from the wardrobe.

The Spanish monk nodded and rushed out of the guesthouse.

Christophe continued. "Besides, should he change, we don't know if her blood will cure or kill him." Once the soiled clothing was stripped off, the abbot pointed to the water bucket sitting off the side of the fireplace. "How clean is that water?"

The young woman answered. "It's barely been used. Brother Marcos fetched it earlier today."

"Excellent. Take it to his room. William, help me carry him to his bed. Henry, burn the robes in the fireplace. They are polluted with Caliss's evil."

27

Fighting Evil with Evil

Abbot Christophe took the cloth and began wiped away some of the still wet blood glistening in the candlelight. Daniela nervously approached the bedside and met the monk's half lidded hazel eyed gaze, following her every movement. Ever since William left to get his medical supplies from the infirmary, Julian hadn't stopped watching her. Standing next to her was Henry.

She shamefully peeled her gaze away from the sick's and questioned the working abbot. "How many times have you done this?"

Christophe wrung out the blood stained cloth in the bucket of water. "Done what, my child?"

"This." She gestured at the man lying in the bed, his chest and parts of his body caked with his own blood. "Apparently it's not the first time, seeing how you knew what to do."

Christophe nodded. "Aye, I have seen my fair share of vampire victims through the years. Some were lost, some were saved."

Trying to be as gentle as he could, the abbot blotted at a spot of damp blood near the bite mark. This caused the younger man to tense up in reaction and groan in pain.

Daniela's heart sank and breath seized in hearing the wiser man's statement. "When you say lost, do you mean changed or . . . lost as in—"

"Lost as in changed and killed. Anytime, anyone of them was successfully changed, I found it my duty to rid the world of their damned souls."

Christophe wiped clean the rest of Julian's neck, and peered into the desperate and quiet plea of the younger man's eyes. There was something there the abbot had never seen before. He took hold of the monk's hand with a strong, but comforting grasp. The gesture was returned, leaving Christophe surprised. For someone in such a weakened state, Julian had a surprisingly strong grip.

Julian's brow weakly twisted in an almost silent plea for help. He didn't want to die; not like this. He knew all too well the sometimes brutal and heartless acts of the abbot to those who had fallen victim to evil's influence. He could see himself sharing the same fate as the others and this scared him. His life was now in the hands of one of the church's most esteemed warriors.

The abbot gave a sideways glance at the young woman and spoke in a demanding voice. "Leave us, child. Wait for Brother William outside."

Daniela's mind raced with confusion. "Abbot?"

"Do as I say, child." His full attention rested solely on the Daniela. "Brother Henry, you stay. I will certainly need your assistance."

The piercing gaze Daniela was receiving from the man unnerved her, a bit. It was as though he were someone completely different. Nodding once in acknowledgment of the order, the young woman did as told and backed away toward the door. A part of her knew leaving the two men alone would end in horrible consequences, but who was she to argue with the abbot?

Christophe returned his worry stricken gaze back down on Julian and pressed his lips together in skepticism.

The monk was barely able to speak, his voice a raspy whisper. "W-what are you going t-to do?" Julian painfully swallowed. "You're n-not going to k-kill me . . . are you?"

Christophe placed a hand on the man's forehead and shook his head. Just like all the other victims in the past, this young man had the same abnormally high fever. Seeing this monk before him as he was, was heartbreaking.

Yet, Christophe smiled a sympathetic yet reassuring smile. "No, no, my son. I'm going to save you." Tears were beginning to pool behind the levees of his lower eyelids. "You will soon walk with the guardian angels of heaven's damned children." Christophe studied Henry and softly spoke. "Lock the house door. I must not be interrupted."

Henry sympathetically frowned to Julian and did as ordered.

*   *   *   *

Outside, Daniela's watch ripped away from the infirmary's direction, expecting William's return, and to the door in alarm. She reached for the handle and jiggled it, finding it locked. She knew she shouldn't have left Julian's side and began throwing her body into heavy oak door in hopes of opening it.

Julian watched the abbot sit there, for a moment, motionless where he sat.

Christophe could hear the door rattle on its hinges rattle in protest. Gray eyes met the monk's fearful glossy hazel ones. In great debate with himself, Christophe heaved a labored breath and wrapped a hand around his cross necklace.

Julian looked between Henry and the abbot. What was he about to do and should he be concerned? "Abbot . . . ?" Had the monk had any more strength, his words would've been on the brink of hysteria.

The highly esteemed, religious figure questioned in a hushed voice. "Do you trust me, my son?"

The monk always trusted Christophe, for he had more looked up to him as a father figure. But at this moment, he wasn't sure anymore. Without thinking, the word, "Yes," slipped from his trembling lips.

"Good." Christophe hung his head low and closed his eyes. He began to whisper what could easily be made out as prayer from over the loud banging of the door. Moments painfully ticked by as Daniela's frantic banging on the door was replaced with mournful sobs.

*   *   *   *

The abbot glanced down at the monk with a bloodshot stare. The look in those usually gentle eyes had now been replaced with something inexplicably appalling.

Julian's breathing became further labored. Since figuring out the abbot's secret, a part of him always worried if it would later become a threat. He tried to yell for help, but it was no use. His voice was a hoarse whisper of a cry and barely strong enough to register past this throat. The monk helplessly watched from the older man close in on him. Those inhuman eyes were a crushing weight to the monk's already debilitated body. As if breathing wasn't difficult, as is, it was now downright impossible. Still, Julian tried to cry for help; to beg mercy of his executioner.

"Shhh . . ." The abbot placed a hand on the monk's mouth and closed his eyes, taking in another deep breath.

He allowed the smell of the fresh blood to fill his senses and at releasing the breath, curled his upper lip to reveal elongated canines. Christophe kept his hand on the monk's mouth and spoke, meeting the other's wide-eyed gaze.

"Forgive me, my son, but if I don't do this, your soul will be forever tainted by Caliss . . . and you will know . . . only . . . evil." A whimper of a cry escaped through the fingers of the abbot's hand clutched around Julian's mouth. Tears poured from the monk's eyes and onto the older man's cold, restraining fingers. "Call it an exorcism of the sorts."

Julian couldn't take his eyes off Christophe's. The longer he stared into those nightmarish eyes, the more of a calming sensation began to encase him. Hypnosis. He suddenly remembered his training from the Sect to never look into the eyes of a vampire. Yet, he found himself unable to look away. The pains in his body and acid searing his veins began to give way to a comforting warmth.

Abbot Christophe watched the monk fall into his hypnosis and gently brought his hand from the monk's quiet mouth. He brought it to the back of the man's head and lifted it slightly off the soiled pillow. In regret, he kissed the monk's sweat glazed forehead and neared the cauterized wound at his swollen neck. There was no mistaking the unappealing scent of the venom tainted burnt flesh.

The abbot paused a moment to whisper, "Forgive me, my son," before biting into the feverish man.

Julian's body went into spasm in reaction to the pain streaking through his body. He felt a strong hand plant itself in his chest to hold him still. Silent screams came from his throat as he grabbed at anything his hands would take hold of.

Henry's eyes filled with revulsion and regret, but knew what the priest was doing was for the best.

Christophe could taste the bitter venom of the other vampire's mixed with what remained of Julian's blood. He knew he wouldn't be able to completely remove it from the younger man. Too much had already been absorbed into the body, but the abbot knew in order to save the monk, he'd have to drain him of his remaining, tainted blood source. He dug his fangs deeper into the pulsing vein; the remaining life supply becoming less and less.

Gradually, over time, Julian's grip around the abbot's arm relaxed only to fall limply to the bedsheets below. His entire body was completely lost of feeling and his vision giving way to the encroaching darkness. There was no trying to fight off the vampire's feeding and gave into it in surrender. In his final conscious moments, all he could think about was William and the other monks. How could he have let them down? How could he have let *her* down? After swearing he would protect her until death? And death was closing in on him.

Abbot Christophe felt the life completely diminish from the monk and withdrew his fangs. He met the lifeless hazel eyes of Julian, staring off in the direction of the guesthouse door. Traces of the man's last tears fell from his eyes and glided down his cheeks to join the bloody pillow. Christophe wiped away his mouth and swallowed the remaining bitter blood.

He could feel the acid of the venom tear away at his insides and clenched his jaw in agony.

28

Purging of Evil

William hastily strode up to the guesthouse carrying a wooden bucket steaming with hot water in one hand and a leather shoulder bag in the other. Marcos was accompanying him in carrying a clean robe. They both saw Daniela, a heap of tears curled at the door.

Marcos questioned. "What are you doing out here?"

William set the bucket down and tried to open the door only to find it locked. "Why is the door locked?"

The woman eyes were transfixed on the glow emitting from beneath the door and responded. "Abbot Christophe wanted me to wait outside. I don't know why and I didn't argue the reason. After I left, he locked the door behind me." Her face contorted into sobs of hopelessness. "I tried to bust it down. I was afraid he'd kill Brother Julian, seeing how he was bitten."

William felt his entire body be overcome in sickening dread. He balled a fist and frantically pounded on the door. "Abbot Christophe? Open the door!"

The door unlocked, revealing the troubled older man. First glance proved something was wrong with the abbot. His color wasn't the same as he looked terribly ill. "It's about time," he wheezed. "I tried washing Brother Julian the best I could in your absence." He took the water bucket and went back to the bedside of the seemingly resting monk. "I will be staying in here for the night. I would like to personally look over him for any sudden changes."

William spoke to protest. "But, Abbot, I—"

Christophe cut the other man off in midsentence. "I know what to look for as far as negative reactions to the venom." He sighed in exasperation. "And please, clean up the rest of that mess in the living area. It's an eyesore and greatly offends me."

William leaned out of the room and into the living area where the crimson mass on the floor stared back. "I'm sure I can find some extra rags and a mop to clean it up with."

Again, the man left. Daniela refused to leave the guess house, this time, and stood along the wall behind the abbot. Marcos, still having a job to do, stood protectively next to her.

Christophe winched and squeezed his eyes shut at the pain burning in his stomach. Thankfully the young woman couldn't see his face, right now. He groaned to her, "I advise you leave, dear girl. Go . . ." his clenching his jaw cut off his words, momentarily. "Go help Brother William."

The young woman shook her head. "I won't leave."

"*Now!*" The order was more growled than said and it startled the already nerve wracked woman into fleeing. Marcos, too, was shaken by the outburst and followed the young woman in escort.

The heavy wooden door of the house closed behind them, Abbot Christophe seizing in spasm. He had a feeling this would happen and though in acute pain, gladly accepted it for the possible chance at Julian surviving. The man doubled over, wrapping his arms around his midsection as he fell from the bed and onto the floor. A snarl escaped his throat and he desperately clawed at the frigid, stone floor, fangs bared and eyes squeezed tightly shut.

Henry was by his side, willing to offer whatever assistance was needed. "What do you need me to do?"

Christophe knew the poisonous venom of Caliss was starting to absorb into his body. Before the sickness could completely consume him, he'd have to purge his body of the toxin. He would not let himself fall to the corruption of evil he had shelled within him. Never had he experienced such intense pain like this. The closest to it was when created by the very demon he swore to kill.

"Help . . . me," whined the terribly ill abbot. "The fireplace . . . help me . . ."

Barely able to sit upright, let alone stand, the priest was almost carried to the living area. He could see the fire lit hearth and strained himself to reach it. Another spasm wrought his body into muscle jolts and he hoarsely whimpered out loud. He pushed Henry away and painfully fell to his knees.

Christophe began to gag and choke in the urge to be sick. Desperate to rid his body of the corruption within him, he started vomiting thick blood streaked with black. Henry felt himself gag and quickly looked away, bringing a hand to his mouth.

*　　*　　*　　*

Caliss roared out and ripped away his blood stained clothing, revealing his newly obtained injuries. Five of his followers recoiled in fear of their master's rage as he stumbled through the ruined town's butcher shop cellar. He effortlessly tossed a meat trimming table against a wall and almost hit a couple of followers.

The enraged vampire slammed a fist against the mantle above the fireplace, alive with flames, and sneered. "I want that girl!" His body convulsed in a spasm and he momentarily faltered in an overwhelming burning sensation that stemmed from the gash as his neck and shoulder. "And I want that damn monk *dead!*"

A lightly armored, and obviously terrified vampire follower, came into full view from his standing on the cellar stairs. "What of Christophe, my lord? He will be no easy task on his own."

Caliss forcefully swallowed Julian's remaining blood in his throat and licked at what had seeped from the corners of his mouth. "Leave the old man to me."

The armored vampire took a cautious step toward his leader. "But, my lord, Christophe's power mirrors your own. To take him alone would—"

"The priest's strength wanes and he know it." Again, Caliss loudly groaned behind fang bared, clenched teeth and clawed at the wood of the oak mantle. "Even now, he tries to fight it, but he will not succeed." The vampire collapsed to the stone floor and howled in pain. "I . . . will . . . have that girl!"

Around the cellar and creeping down the stairs, several vampires could see one of the most powerful vampires in existence be overcome by an unknown force. It was something they had never seen and they began to wonder, exactly, just how strong he was. Almost as though sensing their doubt, Caliss glared over his shoulder and over to the armored vampire, growling.

The vampire took a step back, intimidated by the fire-glazed bloodshot eyes of Caliss staring back at him. "M-my lord?"

A flash of movement was all the room's occupants saw as the partially bloody vampire charged to his devoted follower. The man became paralyzed in his master's un-relentless, single handed grip around his jaw and whimpered.

The blond long-haired vampire tugged at the man's face so their faces were now inches from the other and growled, "I will not be made an example of."

His grip tightened around the lesser vampire's face, Caliss baring his fangs beneath his curled, upper lip. The distinct sound of the vampire's jawbone snapping followed by a scream of stabbing pain pierced the cellar air. Fearing they would be next in the rage induced assault, the on looking vampires shrieked and hissed, running for the stairs. With a final, crushing compression, Caliss completely broke the vampire's jaw and tore into his neck with his fangs.

The once piercing screams of the follower became drowned out gargles from blood spurted out of his mouth.

With his other hand, Caliss grabbed a handful of his victim's hair and jerked the head back. Still, the vampire continued to gnaw at the other man's neck, lowering both the paralyzed body and his own to the stone floor, where a pool of blood began forming beneath the two.

With another harsh yank of the man's head, his neck snapped in a series of bone grinds and crunches only to be severed from the neck a moment later. Caliss shot his attention upward from behind several strands of blood drenched hair and hissed a growl to the scrambling vampires.

* * * *

Christophe wearily shuffled into Julian's room and in holding onto Henry's arm, slowly sat down on the bedside. He wiped his sickened lips as beads of sweat ran down his trembling face. Since purging himself the tainted blood, the convulsing spasms had passed, leaving his breathing slow and arduous. His lazy gray eyes examined the peaceful form of the still blood caked monk's body and frowned.

His voice was barely audible in his speaking. "Burn the evil, Henry. The others . . . they must not see it."

Henry took one of the many candles sitting on Julian's nightstand hesitantly left the abbot's side. He went into the living area and in standing feet away from the revolting puddle of blackened blood, tossed the candle in it. Flames erupted from the source and filled the house with its burning stench.

Christophe could smell it and sighed a difficult breath. "Now . . . let's get you cleaned up."

After several minutes of washing most of the dried blood from the monk's neck and partial chest did William, Daniela and Marcos return. Marcos opened the door, watching William's bucket slosh water onto the floor.

Behind him, the young woman emerged into the room as well, carrying a bucket of her own in one hand with a mop in another. Daniela's nose wrinkled to the atrocious smell in the air. "What is that smell?"

Henry emerged from Julian's rooms, responding. "That would be the smell of evil."

Marcos pointed his spear tip to the charred spot on the stone floor in front of the fireplace. "And that?"

Henry wasn't sure how to answer. "Evil comes in many forms, Brother."

The two quietly studied each other, the Spaniard knowing there was more than what was being said. He, William and Daniela began to scrub the floor as Christophe watched from Julian's doorway. His gray eyes kept shifting between the distraught woman and the lifeless form of the motionless monk. Julian seemed like a promising member of the church, Christophe hoping his decision of choice was the right one.

29

Waking into Hell

Valrae descended down the cellar stairs of the butcher shop, her pale green eyes examining the crudely dismembered corpses lying in pools of blood around the floor. She raised a brow in interest and sighed in disappointment. Paying no mind to the gore she sloshed through, she strode over to where Caliss sat on the floor facing the fireplace. Inside it where multiple fanged skulls staring back out of their charred, empty sockets.

She stood beside him and ran her fingers through his still partially blood dampened locks and cocked a smile. "Had a party and didn't bother letting me know?"

The vampire brought a hand to the woman's caressing his head and tightly wound his fingers within hers. "I will not tolerate anyone's questions or doubts over my abilities or power."

"As you shouldn't, my love." She knelt beside the shirtless vampire and focused her gaze on him. With a gentle hand, she turned his face to face. She un-clung several strands of his long hair away from his blood caked face and smiled. "Anyone who dare defy you deserves worse than death."

He caressed her cheek with the back of his hand, leaving a streak of blood in its wake. In analyzing her features, he ran his thumb over her lips and coated them in red. She could taste it and took one of his fingers into her mouth, sucking away the flavorful coating. Caliss emitted a low growl and closed his eyes against the sensation of feeling her fangs brush against his finger. He created her and just as he did, he could kill her and she knew it.

He withdrew his hand from her mouth and pulled in her for a kiss.

The rich taste of blood in his mouth sent her over the edge and she pulled away, sucking and licking at his blood coated jaw and neck.

Caliss brought his hand to her stomach, where he began caressing up the woman's body and over her chest. He closed his eyes against the pleasurable feeling and snarled again, moving his hand to her neck.

In a paralyzing grasp, he now held the woman by her jaw and growled into her ear. "I will not accept failure either, especially from you."

He jerked her face to meet his, the woman drawing her blood smeared lips to bare her fangs at the man with a hiss. "You dare kill me?"

His grip now tightened around her jaw more, just shy of breaking pressure. "You have served me well thus far, my Valrae. Do not let me down." She released a snarl in protest to his hurting her. Caliss released his grip on the woman and pitched her to the carnage littered, stone floor. "Now get out of my sight."

Valrae barked a hiss and crawled away from the angered vampire and to the stairs. Once out of the cellar, the irritated woman gave a hateful glare in the direction she just came from and left the butcher shop.

*   *   *   *

The next morning came early for the monastery. Heavy eyed monks gathered around the burn pit to put to rest their fallen, Brother Luke and Brother Mathew. No one spoke of the events from the night before. Even William didn't say anything that morning. His mind was elsewhere and not paying attention to the world around him. He felt sick and numb all over.

Inside the guesthouse were Daniela, Henry, and Marcos. She sat in front of the fireplace, knees drawn to her chest and head resting atop of them. Marcos sat at the table behind her and thumbing along the blade of his spear lying on the tabletop. Henry had brought a chair from the center table into Julian's room and sat there, nodding off. He would jerk awake in hearing the littlest of sounds and when seeing all was well, would sit back down and eventually nod off.

Once the burning ceremony was over, the ashes of the burned were buried in silver lined boxes. Abbot Christophe wanted to take no chances with both bodies, even though only one of them showed signs of being bitten. More like mauled and barely identifiable.

Christophe dismissed the monks to begin their day and solemnly strode back to the guesthouse. He entered the house and went to check on Julian. A throwing knife whizzing past his face and impaling itself in the room's wooden door stopped him from proceeding. His physically drained eyes shifted from the knife in the door and to the startled and blushing monk sitting in the chair.

Henry had his hands to his face in realizing how close he was to hitting the abbot. "My apologies, Abbot."

The older man gave him a stern, but comforting glare. He reached up to extract the blade from the door. "At least your reflexes and aim are unaffected by your lack of adequate rest." He handed the knife back to the monk, Henry accepting it with a shaking hand and stashing it back within his sleeve's concealment. "How does he seem to be doing?"

By now, Daniela had gotten up to join the returned abbot and hear what he had to say. Across the room on his bed, was Julian, still lying the same way he was from the night previously. The pale color of his face paired with the lack of a rising and falling of his chest in breathing greatly showed him to be bead. But the feverish touch of his skin gave hope of his still being alive and possibly living through the traumatic ordeal.

Henry answered. "Resting."

Christophe glanced over his shoulder and to the nerve wracked woman. "Have you managed to rest, even in the least?" She shook her head. Nodding in his, the older man frowned. "Its best you try and get some sleep, my child. You will be needing your strength."

Knowing she was being dismissed, she gave a final look to Julian and went to her room, closing the door. Marcos quietly watched her and heavily sighed.

Christophe felt a hand of Julian's forehead, finding it still feverish, and frowned. "Henry, please close the door. I have something I need to discuss with you." Once the door closed did the abbot proceed. He reached into his robes to disclose a rolled up piece of tattered parchment. His passed the parchment to Henry with a lightly trembling hand. "I found these on Bother Mathew when preparing his body for the burning ceremony."

Henry unrolled the parchment and read over the crude writing. It was nothing like that of any monks' elegant writing. This had been quickly scribbled. "What is this? Who wrote this?"

"My best guess is Caliss." Both men stared at the other in heartbreaking realization. "It seems he was in league with him. He openly invited the vampires and their leader into the monastery and into whatever room they pleased. That . . . that was how Valrae got into this house. It was how Caliss was able to go where he pleased after being snuck in."

Henry thought back on the night before and how he had seen the other carry arms full of dirty robes to the wash house. "That would explain what he was doing working so late, last night." Christophe arching a brow insisted he continue. "I was finishing up in slopping the pigs when I came across Mathew taking the dirty robes to be washed in the morning. I thought it a bit suspicious he being out so late, but didn't press the matter. It's not uncommon to find him out and about in the oddest of places during whatever hours doing something. Like the time he was out before morning prayer and trimming the hedges."

Henry handed the parchment back to Christophe, the older man setting it aside on the nightstand. "Alert me when he wakes . . . if he does at all." With that, he rose to his feet and left the guesthouse.

"But . . ." Henry leapt to his feet. "Should he wake, wont he . . . I mean after last night he'd be a—"

Christophe didn't verbally answer but his glare was answer enough. The monk nodded in acceptance and sat back down in a plop. The morning sun shone through the opening door for a brief moment before the dim light of the house returned in its closing.

Henry wrapped a hand around his cross necklace and began to pray.

*   *   *   *

Christophe stood under the covered walkway of the vegetable garden, just shy of the morning sun's rays. He watched as three monks did their morning manual work post midmorning prayer and thought to himself. If one person slipped by his detection in working with the evils outside the monastery walls, then how many more were too?

The abbot frowned in disappointment. If not corrupt now, then how many more would turn their backs on him and their brethren if given an opportunity.

Christophe gazed back over his shoulder and in the direction of the guesthouse across the monastery grounds. A slight smile spread across his features as he whispered to the empty air, "Good morning, my son."

Something in the air smelled differently. His entire body felt different all over. Julian's eyes fluttered open and he strained to focus through the candlelight to look around his room. His whole body ached as he instinctively reached for the inflamed gash on his neck and whimpered.

Henry heard the whimper and almost fell out of the chair.

Julian fought to sit up, but found his body incapable of doing so as the echo of a hoarse moan filled the room. He cried in pain and reached for the bite mark once more as he began to recall a faint memory of the night before.

Henry was hesitant to go to the man's aid and brought a hand to his neck, gulping. He questioned. "B-Brother Julian?"

A knock came on the guesthouse's door. Marcos got up and answered it to find the monastery overseer. "Abbot? Why are you knocking?" His next words were said without knowing what it was he was truly saying. "You are *always* welcomed within these walls."

Though it seemed like a kind, welcoming gesture to him, for the abbot it brightened his features in a weak smile. "Just the words I was hoping to hear." Now that he could come and go at his leisure, he felt greatly alleviated. He went into Julian's room and in opening the door, faltered in smiling.

The abbot closed the bedroom door behind him spoke in a calm voice, hoping to ease the waking monk. "It's all right. I won't hurt you."

Julian groaned again and weakly pushed himself to a more upright position. "Like hell. I remember what you did to me, last night." The monk looked to Henry and then back to the older man. "What did you do to her? I swear if you hurt her I'll—"

"I did nothing, but put her mind at ease to allow for a more restful sleep." Christophe sat on the side of the bed, finding Julian try to scoot away. He failed, however, when waves of pain overcame him. "You're much too weak to try and move. Give it a couple days and you should be able to get around, better. Maybe even after a good feeding, hmm?" The abbot observed Henry recoiled in the far corner of the room. "I think it's time we slaughter one of the pigs, don't you think?"

Henry knew those suggestive words and nodded. It was something he was often told as a hint for fresh blood. "Aye. I know just the one. I'll be back, shortly, with a jug."

"Be quick about it, Brother."

30

Strength and Forgiveness

Henry watched the last of a dying pig's blood fill a third, clay crafted jug. He corked it and left two other monks to finish what he started in butchering the now dead pig. No one questioned why the man corked any animal's blood in a jug. Christophe had once explained it as being to prevent the ground from being saturated with blood that would later draw in vampires. After an experiment done by the Sect, it was discovered a vampire could smell a drop of blood several miles away.

Henry strode around the monastery and back to the guesthouse. He knocked on the door with his foot and quickly got an answer. Marcos, spear in hand and at the ready, opened the door to allow the fellow monk entry. He saw the jugs in the man's arms and was very tempted to question him. Weren't those the same type jugs used for disposing of animal blood post butchering?

Henry could see the flicker of question in the other's chocolate brown eyes. He nervously laughed and tried to explain the jugs the best he could. "Abbot Christophe asked me to get Brother Julian some water. Better it be stored in these jugs to prevent contamination."

Marcos didn't look convinced, but nodded in acceptance of the answer anyway. He returned to where he had been sitting and groaned in exhaustion. He could really use a nap, right now.

Henry entered Julian's room and shut the door behind him. "Fresh delivery."

Christophe took one of the jugs and uncorked it. Julian watched the older man pour the thick, red liquid into a cup retrieved from the living area. He held the cup to Julian, speaking. "I would advise you start off slow to allow your system to adjust to the change in diet. Otherwise, there will a hell of a mess for Brother Henry to clean." The monk watched the cup be outstretched to him. The potent smell of fresh blood surprised him. "What are you doing?"

"You need your strength, my son."

Julian shook his head. "No, I'm not like you. I'm not a . . ."

Christophe raised his brow and deviously smiled. "A vampire?" He pointed to the other's slightly elongated canines. "Then what do call those?"

The monk brought a hand to his teeth, feeling abnormal points of forming fangs. "This isn't happening." He shook his head again in growing hysteria. "I'm not a monster."

"No, you're not. You're different like the very few of us who are." Gray eyes met bewildered hazel ones. "There are those who follow the beast within them and others who choose to overcome it. If you were a monster, you would have attacked Henry after waking."

Julian looked over to the monk sitting the jugs on the floor by the abbot's feet. Fear crossed the younger man's face. "How do you hide it?"

Christophe patted the man's shoulder and gave it a light grasp. "That's not wine I'm drinking at dinner, just so you know." The monk was confused as he ran his tongue over his new forming fangs. "Now, unless you plan on explaining to everyone why you have those, you might want to satisfy your hunger."

"Why can't I just eat breakfast like everyone else?"

Henry sat down in the chair he had been occupying and faintly smiled. "Breakfast has come and gone, dear brother."

Christophe gave a sympathetic smile to the man before him. "For the first few weeks you will still crave mortal food but, unfortunately, will be unable to enjoy it the way you once could."

"But, you eat with us during meal times."

The abbot nodded in acknowledgment. "Aye, that I do, but it has taken me nearly two hundred and fifty years to learn how to reacclimate my body to digest food."

The monk reached out and accepted the offered cup and paused, the scent of the fresh blood further filling his nostrils. Falling to his new desire, Julian brought the cup to his lips and took a sip. He expected to be sickened by it by it, but found he wasn't. The still warm liquid running down his throat urged him to drink more. He had to have it. He thirsted for it and ached to fill himself.

Christophe eased back on the cup to momentarily stop the other in his drinking. "Easy. Allow your body to adjust to it."

The monk spoke, a half smile threatening the corner of his blood coated lips. He licked away at its sweetness and wasn't aware he was subtly growling. "Is it always like this?"

Christophe lightly nodded and replied. "Unfortunately, yes." The older man studied his new student, who drank more from the cup until empty. "How do you feel?"

Julian sat and thought for a moment, huffing a laugh to himself. "Much better."

"Feel sick, any?"

Julian shook his head. "How will I know if my body isn't adjusting to . . ." The man paused at the thought of him now having to resort to consuming blood.

"You would know immediately. Seeing how you seem fine, you're adjusting well." Christophe analyzed the younger man's teeth to see the growing fang tips still showing. "You could use a bit more. The way you know your hunger has been satisfied is when your fangs retract. With practice, you will learn how to be in control of them and can freely extend them as you please without being in a blood hunger."

Julian hastily drank another cup poured for him and didn't stop till all was gone. "More," he urged.

Henry shifted nervously in his chair. "Abbot, how much should he consume?"

"Let me worry about that, Brother," the older man responded. He poured a third cup and handed it to the thirsting, younger man.

Hazel eyes were turning bloodshot and the monk's growling becoming louder in impatience. After a jug and a half's worth of blood was consumed did Julian cease in his quenching the conjoined thirst and hunger.

Christophe saw the other's hunger induced bloodshot eyes return to normal, but the fang points still noticeable. He worried how this was going to go, should someone notice, and how could they not? New vampires had no control over their fangs. It took him years to learn how to control his and that was something Julian did not have. He was in a monastery, surrounded by several monks trained in combating vampires. How would they react, knowing one of their own brethren was what they had been trained to eradicate?

What would they do if they knew he, their beloved abbot, was one? Would they turn their backs on them or embrace them?

Christophe shifted his gaze's direction to the sidewall and toward Daniela's room across the guesthouse. "She'll be waking soon. I advise you get some more rest. Trust me, you'll feel much better when you wake after feeding."

The older man rose to his feet, Julian questioning. "Will I crave her blood too?"

Christophe nodded. "If anything, you will crave it more seeing how you crave more from her then just a friendly conversation." Faded blush filled the monk's cheeks. "No sense in telling you to not fall into the lust of flesh, hmm?" Julian weakly laughed. "If anything, try to get some exposure to her. I'm curious to know how she smells to you."

The monk blinked in confusion. "What?"

"A warm, honey scent or a pungent vinegar could very well determine what consuming her blood would do for you." The monk lay back against the pillow and fell quiet in thinking. "Brother Henry, do keep a close eye on Julian. Should he shows signs of aggression, you know what to do."

Julian and Henry observed the other in uncertainty, the heavyset monk tucking his hands within his sleeves. Julian knew this wasn't to keep his hands warm and subconsciously hissed a low growl.

31

Acceptance

Daniela rolled over to get more comfortable in her bed, not wanting to wake up. In remembering the night before, she fervently began feeling her neck. She sighed in relief. Julian. He had been bitten and she leapt to her feet to check on him. Her bedroom door being jerked open startled Marcos awake.

He had nodded off in his chair, at one point. His head was leaning against his spear, propped up on a second chair.

Hearing the suddenness of a door be opened made him habitually swing his spear out the hurried movement in the corner of his eye. "Watch out!" called Daniela, throwing herself to the floor to avoid being struck.

Impacting a solid form stopped the spear in its path. Brown eyes looked to a hand tightly gripping his spear's shaft and followed the arm upward to meet infuriated hazel eyes. The Spaniard's jaw fell agape and his eyes widen in speechless shock.

Daniela looked to the rigid form of Julian standing protectively over her and too, fell wordless. Her eyes went to the swollen, red bite mark shining against the monk's still pale and clammy skin.

Julian spoke, his eyes slimming down and jaw clenched. "Might want to take better precautions on who you're about to attack."

Marcos stammered. "A-after last . . . last night, I—"

Julian shoved the spear away from he and Daniela's direction, Henry not sure what to do. He couldn't attack Julian, through showing some form of aggression, because of his protecting the young lady. He twirled one of his smaller throwing knives in his right hand's fingers while anxiously tapping on his left leg's thigh with his other hand.

Hazel eyes downcast to the appalled green eyes staring up at him. He remembered what the abbot had told him and kept that forward in his mind. "Are you okay?" He held out a hand for the young woman to take in assisting her to her feet.

No sooner to her feet than tightly hugging the man. "I was afraid you weren't going to make it."

Julian embraced the woman in his arms and deeply inhaled her scent. Natural warm honey. The warmth of her neck brushed against his much colder cheek and he lightly shuddered because of. His insides pained in desire and he drew her away from him before he did something he'd regret.

The woman glanced around, hoping to find Abbot Christophe, but didn't. "Where's Abbot Christophe? I figured he, if not Brother William, would be here."

Julian looked to Henry. "Will." He rushed past Henry and to the guesthouse door to find the brilliance of sunlight outside. Even though new to vampirism, knew better than to go outside in the sunlight.

Henry grabbed him by the shoulders. "Brother, you mustn't over exert yourself. You should still be in bed . . . resting . . ." He gave a comforting pat to the other man and looked over to Marcos. "Can you please find Brother William and have him sent here?"

Marcos shook his head. "I'm not leaving Miss Daniela's side."

Henry anxiously laughed. "It's daylight out, Brother. Vampires do not wonder about when its sunlight. She will be fine."

The Spaniard looked between Julian and Henry and nodded to oblige. He knew the woman was in good hands with Henry around. Not to mention the abbot treating Julian post being freshly bitten. Seeing how he was up and about and not trying to tear at their throats must be a good sign the treatments worked.

Julian looked back at Daniela and visually searched her for any obvious injuries. He brushed aside her hair on either side of her neck to check for any bite marks and faintly smiled in not finding any.

She took his hands in hers and gave him an odd look. "Your hands are absolutely freezing."

The monk laughed off the comment. "In case you forgot, I was attacked by a vampire. It's going to take me some time to recover."

Daniela escorted the man to the fireplace and motioned him to sit down with her. "Let's try to warm you up, then. You being so cold doesn't feel right." She kept his hands in hers and rubbed them together to warm them up. "How are you feeling, by the way?"

"Tired and weak, but better than I was last night lying in a pool of my own blood." His words left his lips without thinking. The young woman gasped and looked away from the man next to her. Her hands tightly clenched his and her eyes start to gloss over with tears. "My apologies, my lady, I shouldn't have said that."

"It's fine." She tried to smile the best she could for the man's sake.

He knew better and peeled his hands from hers. He took a seat behind her and ran his hands through the loose, slightly unruly strands of brunette hair. Usually she kept her hair neatly brushed and pinned up in a bun. Not at the present time. His cold touch found its way to the base of her neck and across to her shoulders.

His lips brushed across her ear when whispering, "You're always so tense."

Julian started massaging her shoulders and neck, feeling her pulse beneath his hands. He brushed along her neck with his finger tips and to her jaw. His massaging the muscles, there, encouraged her to lean her head back and against his shoulder. Her natural, sweet honey scent was borderline overwhelming for the man. He trailed up her neck in light kisses and paused at the vein, enticing him to bite. His upper lip curled and his more so formed fangs become exposed.

He remembered how the pig's blood tasted and though while enjoyable, knew a human's blood would be better. Why else did vampires feed on humans and not animals? There had to be a reason and he deeply breathed in her scent, again.

Henry's watch shifted from outside the door and to the two next to the fireplace. His heart stopped in his chest. Julian was hovering dangerously close to the woman's neck and appearing as though about to bite her.

Marcos returned to the guesthouse and ran in through the wide open door. He saw Julian and Daniela and noticed the other monk having what looked to be fangs. He shoved past Henry, bellowing, "He's a vampire and you were going to let him bite her?" The young woman's frantic green eyes looked to the fang bared Julian, hissing at Marcos. "Vampires don't need to wonder about, outside, when they're already here . . . *inside*! I knew better than to leave." He raised his spear defensively to the other man.

Henry quickly closed the guesthouse door to avoid any passerby seeing what was happening inside.

Julian and Daniela got to their feet, Marcos's tight hand clasping around the woman's upper arm to pull her behind him. This upset Julian even more. His hissed a growl and everyone jumped back in recoil.

Daniela slid past the protective Spaniard and rested a hand on his spear's blade to lower it.

Her green eyes studied the fang bared monk. "No," she stated aloud to those present. "I trust him."

The words struck the angered Julian and his features start to ease from their upper lip being curled. Every little step the young woman took toward him had everyone that much more on edge.

Once within arm's reach, Daniela brought a hand to the man's face and cradled his cheek in her palm. Julian wrapped her hand in his and nestled into its warmth. He drew her closer to him and comfortingly held her against him.

He softly spoke into her ear. "I would never do anything to hurt you."

The woman squeezed her eyes shut as a tear slid from her eye. "I know."

William was next to charge in through the front door, not expecting Henry to be so close behind it, and ran into him. Both men fell to the floor, William grumbling. He rubbed the part of his head that had hit the stone floor and explored what he could of the guesthouse with fraught eyes.

Standing not far away was his older brother. "You're awake!" William's smile couldn't be restrained. He scrambled over Henry getting up and almost knocked Daniela down in getting to his brother. Not realizing this, he tightly held Julian in a body compressing hug and laughed in joy. "I kept expecting someone to tell me you weren't going to make it!"

Julian spoke through his brother unintentionally smothering him. "For a while, there, I didn't think I was."

Marcos shook his head and mumbled to himself. "You still might not." Henry, standing next to the Spaniard, gave him a stern glare. Dark brown eyes cut down on the plump monk. "Just wait till Abbot Christophe hears about this, about how you almost let him—"

"Hears about what?" William interrupted. He heard the soft spoken comments and questioned under a furrowed brow. "What almost happened?"

Henry cut off anything Marcos was about to say. "How Brother Julian is up and doing well." He didn't have to look over to see the scowl he was receiving from the Spaniard.

William could, however, and became more uncertain. Was there something he was missing? His eyes shot over to his brother, smiling as goofy as ever. This was something he commonly did to hide something. Hazel eyes slimmed in question to the ones staring back at him.

32

The Options at Hand

Christophe had his hood drawn when rushing through the monastery and to the guesthouse. He had received news from a monk working in the kitchen, at the time, of the Julian's requesting to speak with his brother.

Hopefully nothing was going to be said of his undergoing transformation.

Up ahead was the guesthouse and in not wanting to prolong any sun exposed discomfort, the older man darted from the safety of the shadows and through the stream of sunlight outside the house's front door. His clothing had a very light smoke emanating from them by the time he entered the house.

He saw Marcos and Julian standing before the other with their weapons drawn at the other's neck. Sitting at the table with his head between his knees was a flabbergasted William and unconscious on the floor was Henry. Daniela was kneeling beside him and trying to wake him.

Christophe went straight for the two armed monks and bellowed, "*Enough!*" His thin fingers wrapped around one of Julian's sword aimed at Marcos and motioned for it to be lowered. Droplets of blood came from the man's hand pressing against the blade.

Marcos wasn't about to let his guard down. "He's one of them, Abbot! He's a demon!"

Christophe managed to get Julian to lower his swords and resheath them, but rather reluctantly. Still pressing against his neck where his swollen bite mark was, was the spear tip. "What a person has become doesn't necessarily make them a demon." The whites of his eyes were replaced with bloodshot veins and a lip curling upward exposed elongating canines.

Marcos gasped and tears swell in his eyes. "You too? But . . . but when?" The grip on his spear was starting to falter. "In the entire fifteen years I've been serving these walls, I've never once heard of you being bitten."

Christophe eased his defensive posture and flared his nostrils in annoyance. "That's because my transformation was roughly two hundred and twelve years before your being born."

Julian took advantage of the waning grip on the spear and acted quickly. He dropped his sheathed swords to the floor and with his left hand, hit the spear tip upward. He grabbed the shaft with his right hand and had Marcos at spear point. He lightly pressed the tip into the other's neck, just shy of breaking the skin, to prove his point.

William leapt to his feet and fell backward over the chair. Daniela yelled out and brought her hands to her face.

"If I wanted to kill you, I would've done it already," Julian growled. "My being different on the outside doesn't change who I am on the inside." He lowered the spear and shoved it back to its owner. He then rolled his floored weapon onto his foot and kicked it upward to rearm himself.

Marcos accepted his spear and back peddled from the transformed monk. He looked to Christophe. "You're going to allow him to *live*?" He held up a hand to stop whatever answer he was about to receive. "Wait, of course you are." The Spaniard shook his head, laughing in distrust. "You're one of them, so why wouldn't you?"

"Because there is a job still needing to be done," Christophe growled back. "I chose to let Julian live for a reason. I could've killed him, but spared him. Why? Caliss's forces are growing stronger and bolder. Even the son of Lilith himself chanced coming onto holy ground for the blood! It's only a matter of time before he tries again. We need all the help we can get." His eyes, coming off their being bloodshot, focused on Julian. "No matter what form. That being said, I have sent word to the church informing them of the growing dangers and have requested reinforcements be brought in." He sighed. "May I speak with you in private, Brother Julian?"

The younger vampire nodded to older and started to follow him outside. He stopped, seeing the sunlight still shining. "How?"

Christophe tossed his hood back over his head and drove his hands within his sleeves. "Cover what you can of your body and be quick. Since your transformation isn't fully complete, you are less susceptible to the sun's influence. Don't get me wrong, it's still fatal should you linger, but very brief exposure will do nothing more than a bit of sunburn to exposed skin.

Covering your body will lessen the amount of direct sun you receive." The abbot rushed from the house and to the protective shade of the monastery.

Julian gave a final look to those behind him, attention lingering on Daniela, and did the same as the monastery overseer. He used his rope belt to secure his swords to his side and covered his head with is robe's hood. He also made sure his hands and arms were secured in his sleeves. Seeing the abbot walk away, the monk rushed through the sunlight and into the shade to catch up.

They passed two monks in their going to safety and security of the abbot's house. They stood as far against the walls, uncertain of the pale faced monk. The bite mark could be seen beneath the drawn hood and it bothered any who saw it.

Mentor and student went into the private house's living area, Julian shutting the door behind them. Everything was less spacious than the guesthouse. Across the house was the closed door leading to the bed chambers. On either side of the stone walls were stained glass windows peeking over the tops of drawn curtains.

Aside from the paintings of past saints hanging on the walls, there wasn't much for interior decoration. Christophe pulled back his hood and knelt in front of his fireplace to start a fire.

Julian studied the older man. "What's this about? Why the private talk?"

"Do you remember what I asked of you earlier today? About what you smelled of Miss Daniela?" He studied the nodding monk.

"Warm honey."

Features upturned with a scheming smile and Christophe returned to stoking the coals. "Which means one of two things. She'll either make you mortal, again, or empower you. Had you have smelled something resembling vinegar, biting her would most definitely kill you."

"Bite her?" Julian blinked in surprise. "You want me to bite Daniela?"

Christophe got to his feet and stood before the taken aback monk. "Now is the time to defeat Caliss. We have the ability to defeat him, Julian!"

"By doing what, exactly? Bite Daniela?" The monk was curious to know what it was that was going through the abbot's head.

The abbot took hold of the man's shoulders to stare him deeply in the eyes. "She can make you stronger! You can defeat Caliss!"

"I can't do that. I can't bite her! I *won't* bite her!" Christophe's furrowing brow lowered in an acidic glare. "Even if I did, you said there was a chance her blood could also make me mortal. What good would that do?" Julian gave a disbelieving laugh and rubbed his face with his hands. "I don't believe this. The whole purpose of her being here is for protection! You!" Julian poked a finger into the other man's shoulder. "*You* assigned me to protect her! Wouldn't biting her be against protecting her?"

"My assigning you was before you were changed."

The monk shook his head. "No, I won't do it. I refuse to."

Christophe responded in growls. "I will not let Caliss consume the blood, again. You biting her is the lesser of two evils!"

Julian looked in horror at what the highly revered religious figure was proposing. "You won't bite her, yourself, because you know her blood will kill you. She smells of vinegar to you, doesn't she?"

Christophe pushed the younger man away from him in rage. He composed himself in a deep breath. "Trust me, my son, these decisions weren't easy for me to think of. We must do what is best for the church and for its inhabitants within it."

Julian let out a sharp snarl and slammed a fist into a brick wall. "I will not bite her nor will I let anyone else! I swore I would protect her the best I can and I will do exactly that!"

Christophe snarled and narrowed his eyes at the younger vampire. "Refrain from your violent outbursts, Brother Julian, as they get you nowhere." The two men locked stares, the monk seeing something almost sinister in the other man's insensitive glare. "Do what I ask of you or I will rid of the blood to prevent Caliss getting it."

Before Abbot Christophe could take another step closer to the house's door, Julian blocked the way. "You will not harm her."

"Step away from the door."

Christophe tried to gently push the other man aside, but the monk wasn't going to allow it and grabbed the offensive man's hand with a surprisingly strong grasp. In his other hand were his swords. His thumb rolled over the center latch to loosen them for extraction.

The religious figurehead stopped in his tracks and threateningly growled, "You don't want to do this, boy."

Julian didn't verbally answer and narrowed his forming, bloodshot eyes in response. Abbot Christophe jerked the monk's hand on his shoulder and in knowing where to hold the wrist, tightly compressed a pressure point. Julian's grip loosed, allowing Christophe to side step past him.

The monk slung his swords apart with one hand, discarding one to the floor and arming him the other. He held it at the other man's neck, baring fangs and eyes bloodshot.

Christophe caught the back of the younger man's armed hand with his right and grabbed the back of the sword's hilt with his left. He turned Julian's hand over to both loosen the grip and pull it from the other's grasp. In the fluidity of the actions, the abbot had disarmed Julian with the blade in his left hand and now at its owner's neck. Feeling as though he had convinced the monk to decease his protesting, he tossed the sword to the floor.

Julian was determined to stop the abbot and lunged for him.

Christophe painfully seized his attacker by his throat and shoved him against a wall. Grunting a growl, he hoisted Julian into the air as far as his reach would allow.

The older man could see the monk fight for air and deviously smiled in satisfaction. "You have shown great determination throughout your time here at the monastery." He flexed his grip around the man's neck, further choking off his air source. "Given a little assistance with your new abilities, you might just be what I've been hoping to find for a replacement."

Julian felt himself be released and collapsed to the stone floor, desperately gasping and coughing for air.

Christophe gave a final, fanged sneer to the wheezing monk and stepped over him to exit his private house.

The monk scrambled to his feet and stumbled outside to following the priest the best he could.

33

Betrayal

The two people were almost to the guesthouse. Julian saw some of the sunlight had given way to shadow from a setting sun and knew night would soon be approaching.

Christophe knocked on the guesthouse door and Henry answered quickly after. "I need to speak with Miss Daniela. Where is she?"

The monk looked to Julian rushing up behind the abbot. "Don't tell him, Henry!"

Christophe pressed on. "I need to speak with her—now."

Henry recoiled in his reply. "She's not here, Abbot. I'm sorry." Gray eyes turned bloodshot and canine teeth start to draw out. The man pushed his way into the house and deeply inhaled the air. Daniela's signature scent was faint, meaning she was, in fact, not present within the house. "She and Brother Marcos left shortly after you and Brother Julian did to help load the wagon for the settlement food delivery."

A flash of black robes and the priest was gone, striding toward the barn.

Julian looked to Henry. "Find William. Tell him to find Daniela or me and to not let her near the abbot."

"What? Why?" He got no answer as Julian ran off in a different direction to check the barn and stables first.

*   *   *   *

Marcos carried a burlap sack containing grain to the wagon and sat is down in the tail bed. Behind him was Daniela carrying her own sack. Within it was an assortment of leeks, turnips and cabbage.

Marcos turned to get another sack only to be greeted by a shovel hitting him in the face. He fell to the ground, holding his bloodied nose and trying to focus on who it was that hit him. He was barely able to focus on the blurry form before another hit at his head rendered him unconscious.

Daniela heard the sound and thought nothing of it in her pushing her vegetable sack to the back of the wagon. A hit to the back of her head stopped her and too, sent her to the dirt ground.

Looming over her was Brother David, his shifty eyes looking around. He tossed the shovel to the ground and picked up the young woman's limp body.

Julian came around barn just in time to a hooded and horseback monk ride out of the stables on a brown mare. Draped over the front of the horse's saddle was Daniela, appearing unconscious. He yelled in roar, "*Daniela!*" but it was no use.

He wanted to follow; to save Daniela. He rushed to the stables to get his own horse, finding Marcos. The man was lying in the remaining sunlight, making it difficult to get to him. Julian worried for the other's sake and covered his head with his hood and wrapped his hands within each sleeve. He grabbed the other man's feet and started to drag him into the barn's shade. His left hand's sleeve slipped off his hand, exposing his bare skin to the overhead sun.

Julian roared out in pain, but didn't let go of his brother in faith and friend. By the time they were in the shade, the monk's hand was covered in weeping blisters and peeling skin. He saw Christophe round the stables and look over in their direction.

Julian yelled out, "Someone just took her! They rode off on a horse!"

"Who?" The abbot covered his bare skin and briskly ran to the stables. He firmly held the man's face in his hands to meet his gaze.

"I didn't see his face, but they took her!" He pointed in the direction the horseman had ridden off in. "He went that way though."

Christophe visually examined Marcos and listened for a heartbeat. He heard one and felt somewhat relieved. Didn't replace the panic he was feeling for the young woman's being taken.

William joined them, followed by Henry. Both new comers looked at the abbot with disdain in uncertainty to his intentions. William panted in inquiring. "Where is she? Where's Daniela?"

Julian hissed a growl and ran his hands through his hair. "Someone took her."

Christophe spoke, next. "It seems there was more than one mole within the monastery. I know where they've taken her."

All eyes, but William's, fell on the figurehead. The monastery physician was examining the extent of Marco's injuries.

The abbot continued. "There's an abandoned settlement a quarter days walk from here, less than that by horse. Some years back, the settlement fell under a vampire raid. Everyone there was butchered like livestock."

Henry nodded. "I remember that. An assault was ordered on the settlement the next day. Every vampire and those suspected of corruption, there, was slain."

The abbot grimly frowned. "Since then the place was closely watched. I'd venture there during the night to make sure the grounds were empty of anymore unwanted inhabitants."

Julian questioned. "When is the last time you checked there?"

"Four months ago. There were no signs of anyone being there everywhere I looked. I checked every building, every nook a vampire could use for hiding. No footprints in the dirt, no signs of the dust within the hollow walls being disturbed. For eight years the place has been an empty, desolate reminder of what plagues these lands . . . until now."

Marcos started to weakly come to and reached for the source of pain at his head. He could feel two, prominent knots beneath the swollen skin and grumbled to himself.

Christophe moved William aside to question the waking monk. "Who did this? Who took the girl?"

"D . . . David." The Spaniard tried to sit up only to fall back down to the ground. "I don't know what he hit me with, but it was before I could do anything. Completely blindsided me." He looked to Julian's burned and blistered hand. "What happened to you?"

"Trying to help you. Had to drag you out of the sun to do it though."

Marcos massaged his throbbing head and thought on the man's actions. He had personally seen the effects of a vampire exposed to the sun and knew it wasn't a pleasant experience. For someone he had previously been arguing with, and even turning against, to risk that to help him?

He was beginning to rethink his negative opinion of the changed monk. "What do we do now?"

Henry scoffed. "Easy, we go get the girl before she can be bitten."

Christophe and Julian looked to the other in opposing thoughts. The monk growled and bared fangs to the abbot's lowering brow.

William looked to the two men, still greatly bothered by his brother's change. "We might be too late if we wait for the sun to set."

Marcos forced himself to sit up and fought past the dizzy spell trying to send him back to the ground. "We don't wait. We get anyone trained in combating a vampire and go after them."

Henry shook his head. "Bad idea. There's no telling how many vampires there are waiting for us in those ruins!"

William grew angrier. "The longer we sit here, doing nothing, the closer Miss Daniela gets to being bitten . . . To Caliss becoming even stronger." He stood up and squared his shoulders. "I may not be a fighter, but damn it to hell, I'll go after her myself if I need to!" He stormed off, leaving the others behind him.

Marcos got to his feet with the assistance of Henry and Julian. "I'm with Brother William. As soon as I get the barn to stop spinning around . . ."

Julian searched the abbot's gray eyes. "What's it going to be? Save the blood or damn her to a life worse than death?"

Christophe snorted. "Before you attempt to go anywhere, trying to fight, you're going to need your strength." His gaze rolled over to the livestock pens. "Brothers, ready your arms and those who can fight. Take the horses and ride out the soonest you can. You," he looked back to Julian. "I suggest you eat your fill as soon as the sun sets."

Hazel eyes filled with bloodshot and an upper lip peeling back to reveal fully elongated fangs.

34

Lost to the Shadows

Nighttime's darkness swallowed the last of the remaining setting sun's light. Horses carrying weapon and torch-wielding monks stormed the abandoned settlement's ruins. Their riders dismounted and began searching every house and covered building for the suspected vampire invaders. Henry and Jordan followed a series of footprints into a house and went inside. Marcos and William proceeded to check elsewhere.

Six other monks did the same, being in pairs should they find a confrontation. Two of the six chose the butcher shop for their investigation. The forwardmost, an older man wielding a broadsword, proceeded into the building first. Behind him was a man slightly younger and carrying two axes for weapons.

The smell of rotting flesh filled their noses. The younger of the two wrinkled his nose. "I don't know about you, Brother Garren, but something recently died in here."

Garren nodded in agreement. After their searching the primary floor yielded little results, they slowly went down the stairs to the cellar. Both men were repulsed by the overwhelming sickening smell and worse-off sight of torn body limbs and mauled torsos. The younger man retreated up the stairs.

Riding into the settlement were Christophe and Julian. The abbot slid off his horse and looked to the ill-faced monk. "Have you found anything?"

A nod came from the monk. "Yes, sir. There are several bodies torn to pieces in the butcher cellar."

"Sounds like the work of Caliss. He's always preferred the more gruesome slayings of his victims." Christophe narrowed his eyes and visually scanned the buildings. "They must've left last night. He knew we'd come searching for him and that this would be where we'd come."

Julian joined the abbot. "Where else could they have gone?"

"There's a number of villages in the area. Who's to say how many supporters Caliss has there, since he had managed to corrupt two of our brethren. Leave nothing past him. He is very powerful in hypnosis and will manipulate anyone he sees a benefit."

Crashing around in one of the buildings got everyone's attention. Julian ran to the building, looking like someone's livestock barn. A cow's skeleton could be seen through tall grass growing around it.

The side door leading to the outside pen was busted open, a scraggly looking man hissing and darting about to avoid capture. Marcos's voice yelled out, "Will, get down!"

A moment later, a familiar spear was hurled out of the barn and toward the fleeing vampire. The spear impaling flesh and breaking ribs filled the air. Bloodcurdling screams came from the vampire as it fell to its knees. He clawed at the spear point protruding through his chest and saw Christophe close in on him.

His blade flashed in the torchlight and the vampire knew there was no escape. The priest's eyes were bloodshot, fangs bared. He tangled a hand in the other's matted hair and jerked the head upright to face him. "Where is the girl?"

The scraggly vampire laughed through the blood filling its throat. William joined and saw this. "A lung has been punctured. There's not much time before he drowns on his own blood." He arched a brow and rolled his eyes. "If that's even possible, for a vampire."

Christophe sneered, pressing his sword against the lesser vampire's neck. "Which is why, dear boy, the heart must be pierced or the head severed from the body."

Marcos took hold of the spear's butt and twisted it to further agonize his target. "My apologies, Abbot. I was aiming for the heart, but"—he gave a downward jerk of the handle, and the vampire wailed in pain and choked on more blood oozing out of his throat and into his mouth—"the little worm wouldn't stop running all over the place."

Christophe pressed with his questioning. "Tell me where the girl is." The vampire spit a mouthful of blood at the abbot's feet. "Very well." He gave a nod of his head to Marcos. The handle of the spear was twisted again, the vampire's crying out unfaltering. "I can do this all night and well into the next day."

"You'd burn," the vampire slurred out.

Julian looked around to study the many buildings on either side of the main street. "I see plenty of places to hide during the day. I'm sure we can find a suitable location to continue this."

The scraggly creature hissed. "I won't tell you a thing!"

William took his brother's swords from his grasp and unsheathed them, holding both to the speared man's neck like a pair of scissors. "I'll cut your head from your body *very . . . slowly . . .* unless you tell me where your master has taken Miss Daniela!"

Marcos arched a brow to the physician's unexpected burst of anger.

Seeing he was going to get no answer, William began closing the blades around the vampire's neck. One side each of the dual-edged blades started to cut into the skin. Blood started to seep from the cuts, William pausing and cocking his head expecting an answer. Nothing, so he cut a little bit more.

The vampire roared out. "Fine! I'll tell you . . ." He glared upward to Christophe.

*　　*　　*　　*

Daniela whimpered to the ringing in her ears and the painful pounding in her head. She weakly lifted her head and looked around. Not much could be seen in the dimly lit room she was being kept in. Across the room were several candles scattered about the top of a table and not much else. An undistinguishable figure loomed in a dark corner, and she squinted her eyes to focus on it.

She tried to move her arms but couldn't. Tried to scream but couldn't do that either. Her hands and feet were bound in ropes and a rag tied over her mouth to muffle her calls for help. All she could do was squirm against the cold stone floor and sob.

The figure slowly transpired from the shadows. Laughing of a woman's voice flood into Daniela's ears, and the form became more visible. Daniela recognized the redheaded woman as her attacker from some nights back.

Valrae caressed the young woman's tear-sodden cheek with the backs of her fingers and viciously smiled. "Where's your protector now?" Daniela hysterically panted behind the rag tied over her mouth. "Pity the sunlight will render him completely useless."

Caliss entered the room behind her and snarled. "Back away from her." Valrae gave a hiss to the restrained woman and stood up, striding away. "You were supposed to tell me when she woke."

The lady vampire folded her hands behind her back. "I was going to, shortly. I still had a score to settle with her first."

Caliss sat down in front of the frantic woman and smiled in triumph. "There's no sense in trying to call for help. See, the people of this fine town know what's best for them. If you yell, they will not go for help. Doing so would result in punishment far worse than the ten biblical plagues brought down upon them." He ran a cold finger beneath the rag to peel it out of her mouth. "Anything you would like to say in the last moments of being human?"

Daniela cried out. "What are you going to do to me?"

Caliss released a haunting laugh. "Why, make you into a god, of course." He ran a hand through her hair. "Just like my mother did to me all those many years ago. Just as I am saving you, she saved me . . . saved me from a certain death of burning sulfur. Lady Lilith came to me from the shadows the night before the cities I called home were to be destroyed by your God. All I needed to do was drink from her body. I agreed.

"When she cut into her neck, there was no blood. What came from her had the color and consistency of pitch, but a taste far better than any wine I had ever drank. Only three others, including myself, survived that night. There would have been four had one not turned to watch the cities burn. She ultimately turned to a . . . 'pillar of salt,' as it was described." Caliss laughed, his fangs fully visible.

Daniela recognized the story. "You're talking about the destruction of Sodom and Gomorrah." The man didn't verbally answer—only sneered. "That explains a lot. You were already damned to a life in hell even before being changed. Sounds like your bitch of a mother found the perfect candidate for a son."

Caliss's easygoing demeanor instantly changed. He grabbed the woman by her jaw and hoisted her off the floor. Her feet were now freely dangling, and she was unable to do anything to defend herself.

She looked into the menacing eyes of her captor and screamed in feeling his fangs tear into her neck. Her body quaked in spasm, and her blood painted her dress in streaks of red. Her cries became hoarse, and her body started to go limp. All her fears were being made reality as the feasting vampire's venom started to turn her veins black with corruption.

35

Weakened

Blood sprayed into the air and onto the front of William, covering his face. He had cut through the flesh of the vampire's neck and to the vertebrae. No matter how much muscle he put into cutting through the bone, he couldn't.

Marcos titled his head. "Hey, uh, Will . . . do you need some help with that?"

Julian's brow wrinkled in observing his brother. He twisted the blades around and grunted a heave. Another twist and the vertebra was severed. "There," he panted. "Just had to find the gap between the bone sections." The head fell to the ground and rolled to a stop at Julian's feet. Julian gave no attention to the head as he was more distracted by the other man's gore drenched face. William was confused. "What?"

Julian shrugged. "You have some stuff on your face, is all."

"Oh?" William wiped off one of the swords on the spear-impaled corpse and held it up to the torchlight to see his reflection. "Do I?"

"A little. It's not a lot though," Marcos chimed, nodding his head. "Hardly noticeable." He coughed and cleared his throat in the heat of the glare he was receiving from the abbot.

Christophe shook his head, walking away. "Make sure to properly dispose of the body and see to it this graveyard is razed to the ground in flames."

The surrounding monks replied with, "Yes, Abbot," and began doing as told.

Dry wood of the buildings quickly caught fire and soon, the entire settlement was aflame. Located a safe distance from the settlement was the horse mounted team. When nothing remained but smoldering coals glowing in the night did the group ride on. Some proceeded to the next town under Henry's direction while Christophe, Julian and some of the lesser experienced combatant monks returned to the monastery.

Henry's group knew the next town would be inhabited and proceeded with caution. There was no knowing who were and weren't followers of Caliss.

*   *   *   *

Julian sat on the floor of Christophe's personal house. He finished sharpening the last edge of his swords and held it up in the firelight to admire. Closer examination revealed something rather disturbing in the blade. He had no reflection. He could see his clothing, but not his body.

The abbot softly chuckled. "I'm sure I had much of the same reaction when I first saw I no longer had a reflection, either."

Julian lowered the blade to resheath it within the other. "What did you mean when you said replacement? Yesterday . . ."

Christophe's expression took on a serious tone. "My time of leading is coming to a close. The church requested I start finding someone to take over my position. Someone stronger and faster."

Julian shook his head in disbelief. "I haven't been this way very long and am still very weak compared to you. Not to mention inexperienced. Having only five years' time served with the church doesn't help, any."

"You're weak at the present time because you're on holy ground. That, alone, greatly weakens a vampire. I have learned to adapt to the strength loss. Once you're out of these walls and off sacred ground, your strength, agility . . . enhanced senses . . . all that will increase. You have a lot of potential, my son. I'm not looking for an immediate replacement. Just one to consider for training. Given some years work and instruction, you will fit the job."

Julian shifted where he sat to observe the other man. "What of the Sect? What will they do to me when they find out I'm different?"

Christophe stretched out in his chair and folded his hands over his chest. "I'm hoping allow you to prove your worth as they did me."

The monk accepted the answer and looked down at his prized weapon. "What of Daniela?" Hazel eyes met gray ones, the older man frowning.

"Given Caliss's desperation to obtain the blood for himself, I fear it might already be too late for her." He could see the other's heartbreaking in slowly closing eyes and sinking head. "He will, no doubt, be empowered and much harder to fight."

"You mentioned sending word to the church for reinforcements." Julian's head lifted back up to intently study the abbot. "When will they arrive?"

"London's should arrive here within the week. As for Abbess Frances, if she and her sisters travel nonstop," he paused, shrugging. "Tomorrow morning the earliest. Come sundown, for sure."

"If we wait that long to do anything than it will surely be too late for Daniela!" Julian growled to himself in frustration at being unable to be of better assistance during the day.

"See this an opportunity for your change to fully complete."

The monk glared at the abbot beneath his wrinkled brow. "My change should already be complete."

"It will feel that way. Trust me, I know. The process takes approximately three days." Mentor and student silently studied the other. "Your body is being completely changed from the inside out. Once it has fully accepted the transformation, you will feel it all over. It's like being born again." The older man smiled.

*   *   *   *

Fire burned in the blackened veins of Daniela. She lay on the wooden floor, eyes reduced to mere slits, and staring off into the distance. An indistinguishable voice filled her head; a voice she had heard before in her past. Trying to move was impossible and highly regrettable. The most she could do without feeling the urge to throw up was move a hand or an arm. Even then, her body would ache with protest. It was though a thousand searing needles were being driven into her body from all different directions.

Her neck felt the worst. Because of the bite's swelling, swallowing was difficult let alone breathing. Each breath in was a raspy wheeze. She felt as though she were suffocating. Another wave of nausea flooded over her as she curled into the fetal position. Why was this happening to her? He said he would protect her, till death. And now, her death was drawing closer. Or was she just now waking from it?

David sat near to where the woman lay and wrung out a bloody rag in a bowl of water. "I don't even know if you can hear me." He gently wiped away the residual blood from the woman's neck. "All of this is for the better though." Her body jerking in convulsing made him stop, for a moment. "Shh, shh, my lady. Rest. You will need your strength in the coming days."

Caliss's subtle laughter came from over David's shoulder. The rogue monk started shaking where he sat, too afraid to look back. He reached for his cross he still wore around his neck and closed his eyes in prayer.

"And yet you . . . still . . . pray." The laughing continued much louder. "Your God abandoned you when you abandoned him."

David opened his tear sodden lashes and gave a final look to Daniela's still barely conscious form. "Forgive me, child." He got to his feet and left the room, leaving the woman and the vampire lord to themselves.

36

Star of Hope

Morning light shone onto Henry and his entourage entering a quiet farming village. Some of the inhabitants working outside saw the approaching monks and looked away as though in shame.

William glanced down at his robes and thought maybe it was because of his appearance. "Perhaps I should've gone back with Abbot Christophe to the monastery."

Marcos snorted a laugh. "You can still go back."

"No," Henry answered. "Brother William's knowledge in healing and medicines might come of use should we find Miss Daniela."

"If it's not too late," William added.

"Keep your hopes up. We don't yet know her fate. She could very well be alive and unharmed."

They rode further into the settlement, Jordan glancing around. His eyes fell on a familiar brown mare tethered to a rope and grazing on a bale of hay. He pointed to it. "Look! It's the horse David stole from the stables!"

Marcos nudged his horse in the sides and urged it to take him to the other. He dismounted and gently pat the mare on the face. He brushed aside a portion of the bangs to see a prominent scar, roughly an inch in length, off center of the forehead.

The Spaniard nodded in confirmation.

Henry studied the many faces of the inhabitants, questioning. "This horse belongs to the monastery from which we hail. The man riding it had a young woman with him he had taken against her will. If any of you have mercy in any of your hearts, you will tell us where either of the two are." There were no answers from the gathering villagers looking solemnly to the other.

William spoke up, next. "In all my years serving the monastery, I have personally seen to the medical care of each of you." His hazel eyes took note of a woman with curly blond hair in a yellow woolen dress. Her hands rested on the shoulders of a little boy. "I helped bring your son into this world. Two years later I tended to him within the monastery when ill with fever." The woman nervously looked away from the monk. "Our walls have done nothing but care for the people of this land. To stand there and tell us nothing when someone knows something is—"

"Look!" An elderly man leaning against a cane pointed down the dirt road leading into the settlement. A horse and its rider could be faintly seen rushing toward them.

Henry's jaw clenched in anger. "David." He kicked his horse in the sides and abruptly rode out of the village toward the approaching figure.

Marcos mounted his horse and joined the other man.

William was about to follow suit, but the blond woman speaking stopped him. "Brother, wait." The monk turned his horse around to face the woman and stared down at her in teetering patience. "The man you spoke of . . . he rode through here last night demanding a horse to continue his journey."

He could see the scowls she was receiving meant she was speaking out of place. The monk pressed her to continue. "The girl? Was she with him? Did he say where he was going?"

"He had a girl with him, yes. As far as where he was going, he didn't say. He took one of the horses and left immediately after."

William looked to Jordan. "See to it this woman and her son are taken to the monastery for sanctuary. The evil silencing these peoples' tongues will no doubt come to punish her." The younger monk nodded. "As for the rest of you," his slimmed down gaze of disgust fell on every other person present. "May God have pity on your souls." With that, he rode off as did the other lingering monks.

Henry could easily recognize the more distinguishable features of the rider and felt more infuriated. Betrayal and the thought of didn't sit well with him. The closer the two got to the other, Henry could see blood stains on his robes. The left side of his face was also streaked with blood from a cut above his right eye. His right hand was tightly holding his left side.

David could see the blurry figures of whom he once called brothers close in on him. They blocked his way, stopping him from riding on, and surrounded him. "Brothers," he weakly stated.

Marcos could see the badly injured man was about to fall off his horse. He pressed the butt of his spear against the other's chest to keep him upright. "Why did you do it? Where's Daniela?"

Henry brought his horse next to David's and reached over to grab the bloody face and turn it toward him. "You took her to Caliss, didn't you?" Faint nodding gave him his answer. "Has he bitten her?" David began to weep. "Has Caliss bitten the girl?"

Quiet sobs distorted the pained features of the injured monk. "Forgive me, Brothers." He fell off his horse, regardless of Marcos's efforts to keep him mounted. William slid off his horse and pushed his way to the fallen monk. He lifted the hand, coated in blood, and saw a nasty gash peek through the torn robes. "When I realized the severity of what I had done, I fled. The vampires," he panted and swallowed the best he could. "They tried to stop me, but it's hard for them to follow when its daylight, outside." He weakly laughed. "I was on my way back to the monastery . . . to warn . . ." David winced at William pressing onto his side to stop the bleeding.

William shook his head. "I can't stop the bleeding."

Henry grabbed David by the collar of his robes and yelled into his face. "Where is Daniela? Where is Caliss hiding? *Answer me!*"

David choked out, "Forgive me," and went limp in the other's clutches.

William leaned in to hear a heartbeat from another, but there was no use. "He's dead."

Marcos traced the dirt road with is eyes as far as he could and flexed his grip on his spear. "He came from that direction which means . . . whatever town or towns are in that direction is where Caliss and Daniela are."

William frowned. "There's no telling which one though. We might have enough daylight to check one more town if we want to get back to the monastery before nightfall."

Henry brought a hand down David's face to close his eyes and shook his head. "We need to get back to the monastery. It took us half the night to get here when we did." His green eyes looked to the horizon Marcos was watching. "Should we try searching the next village, there's no guarantee there would be enough sun to protect us in our return trip. That's not including any possible trouble we might find ourselves in. If that happened, it wouldn't take the vampires long to catch up and overwhelm us." He stood up, eyes now focused on the deceased. "We need to go back to the monastery and relay the news of Miss Daniela's fate to Abbot Christophe. From there, we prepare for the worst."

*　　*　　*　　*

Julian watched rays of the evening sun become smaller and smaller until none were left. He stepped out of the shadows of an arcade and glanced upward to the twilight sky. Overhead, a single star twinkled and he deeply sighed in despair.

Jordan joined him and too, looked to the star. "'Tis a reminder of our purpose." Hazel eyes turned to the teen. "We are that single light, shining in the darkness of present time for others to look up to. That little light refusing to burn out even as everything around us gets darker . . . the star travelers use to find their way when lost." The corners of Julian's lips subtly upturned and a whisper of a laugh escape. "So anytime feeling lost and hopeless, just look to the heavens for that little star of hope."

"And if during the day?"

Both men looked to the other, Jordan smiling wider. "You'd burn," he said without remorse. "The rest of us, well . . . just look for that little sign of hope, no matter what it is." He refocused on the star. "God knows how to speak to the each of us. All we have to do is open our hearts, eyes and ears to his signs, even if it's not what we expect."

"Brother Jordan, that's the best advice I have heard from any man's lips." Jordan blushed and bit back a prideful smile. "Especially from someone as young as yourself. How old are you, again?"

He shrugged. "Seventeen."

The monastery bell ringing startled the two men, them rushing to the monastery's front entrance. They were met by Abbot Christophe appearing just as alarmed as them. "What is it this time?" He saw eight horses stampede into view from the tree line and close in on the monastery. Across one of the horse's backs was a body of a monk.

At first, Julian feared it to be his brother, but seeing William come into view relieved him of that worry. The horseback men rode up to the three awaiting outside the double oak doors, Henry dismounting. "Abbot, we bring news." He gave a respectful nod to the figurehead. "It concerns Miss Daniela . . . and Caliss."

Upon hearing the mentioned name, Julian took hold of Henry's shoulders to stare him deeply in the eyes. "What about her? Where is she?"

"My deepest sympathies, Brother, but," Henry paused, unable to finish his sentence. The heart wrenching guise in the other monk's eyes silenced him of all words.

William continued, dismounting and leading the horse with David's body on the back to the abbot. "She's been corrupted by Caliss." His downcast eyes gestured to the body and back to Christophe. "David told us before his passing to grievous wounds."

The abbot nodded. "Just as I feared. Caliss will stop at nothing to get what he wants." He nodded. "Burn the body and bury the ashes, as per protocol. For the rest of you, prepare for the oncoming battle, as needed."

37

Building Forces

The bell rang in the morning and to a saddening sight. Far off in the distance, pillars of smoke rose to the sky. The death undoubtedly carried with it meant the fall of a settlement and most likely at the hands of Caliss.

Abbot Christophe stood within one of the towers and grimly stared off at the smoke filled horizon. Next to him was Julian and Henry. It was Henry who discovered the ill fate of the settlement.

He frowned. "That looks to be in the direction of the village David came from, yesterday. We were to go there, next, but a gut feeling told me not to."

Julian nodded. "Good thing you didn't too, or it would be your bodies burning to the heavens."

Christophe exhaled a heavy breath. "Best not to ignore the voice of God and his angels."

Hazel eyes remained locked on the smoke clouds. "Why is he doing it? Burning the settlements, that is. Doesn't he know destroying them will reduce the amount of places he can hide? His supporters?"

"Caliss cares for no one, but himself. The settlements he's destroying are him building his forces. He's going to try and take the monastery and the surrounding lands by force of numbers."

Henry gulped. "That sounds bad."

Julian was curious. "Why now? He's had this whole time to act against us."

Henry could see the sunrays creeping closer to the tower and to where the two very vulnerable men stood. His green eyes shifted from the beams

----

and to his companions. Christophe continued. "It's because of me. Caliss knew he couldn't take me as he was on holy ground. He waited till he got the blood to better empower himself. As for his army, having more numbers isn't always a good thing. Quality over quantity, and I'm almost certain Caliss isn't changing all those poor people himself. He's only concerned about biting one person."

"Daniela," Julian growled. "When you say quality over quantity . . . What do you mean? How is he supposed to obtain better quality forces for his army?"

"By biting them himself." Christophe narrowed his eyes down on the younger man next to him. "Weren't you paying attention during your academic training with the Sect?" Julian didn't answer, only sighed. "Ah. You probably suffered the same issue you have during prayer services." Now, the man rolled his eyes in exasperation. "To sum up what you failed to retain, the further from the originating creator's line a vampire is made, the weaker they are in comparison. Take us, for example.

"Caliss himself is responsible for our transformation. Because of his direct involvement, we are almost as half as powerful as he is. Now, say you bite someone. They are now half of your strength and a quarter of Caliss's. That person goes to bite another, who bites another. The last person is a quarter of your strength and far less compared to Caliss." Mentor looked to student. "Understand?"

Julian thought about the abbot's explanation. "If I were to make my own army—"

"Which the Sect would greatly disapprove and probably have you ridden of."

"Hypothetically," the monk added, giving a silent scold to the older man. "It would be preferred I change them all myself . . . for that quality factor, correct?"

Christophe turned to fully face the inquiring monk. "What are you asking, boy?"

"If Caliss is making his own army, what's stopping us from making our own?"

Henry gasped in disbelief. "You can't be serious."

"Absolutely not," the abbot roared. "I allowed your transformation to unfold versus killing you, as I should have, because I knew you would be a valuable ally against the son of Lilith. I will not have you tearing apart these lands just as that demon out there," he aimed a finger at the smoky horizon, "Is doing!" He neared the other, fangs bared and eyes turning bloodshot. "Should you dare try to attack anyone both inside and outside these walls, I will burn you alive myself."

Julian hissed a growl. "If what you're saying is true, that Caliss is building an army . . . What chance do humans stand against mass numbers? Weakened, or not. Those vampires will still be stronger than any amount of reinforcements we have. If even on holy ground."

"What I said remains as is." Christophe growled and lowered his glare on the monk. "Do not make me regret allowing you to live." Turning on his heel, the abbot disappeared down the spiral staircase within the tower.

Henry gave Julian a sympathetic frown. "I suggest you take cover, soon. When the sunlight reaches the tower, there will be nowhere to hide." He gave a gentle squeeze to the other's shoulder and followed the abbot.

*　　*　　*　　*

Daniela's green eyes turning bloodshot watched the sunlight start to fill the bedroom to which she resided. She had been brought here during the night, after Caliss had a handful of his remaining forces annihilate the settlement they had previously been staying in. They were like locusts, moving from town to town and consuming it of its resources. When nothing remained, they moved on to the next.

Why wasn't Christophe or anyone else representing the Sect doing anything? Why were they allowing this to happen? Did they not care now since Caliss had her in his possession?

She tucked a foot closer to her body to avoid the creeping sunlight. The door opening across the room gave way to the house's tenant; a balding, middle aged man. During her being dragged through the house upon arrival posttravel, she had seen the family of four huddled in the corner with Valrae tormenting them. The two young children were terrified and crying. Their mother was trying to comfort them just as the father tried to comfort them all.

She was certain Caliss threatened the family with death if they didn't cooperate as demanded.

The man of the house had a quilt in his hands and he tossed it to the bed. He was jittery around the room's occupant and making sure to keep his distance from her. He withdrew a nail from his saggy brown pants pocket and a hammer from another. In quick work's time, the blanket was nailed over the room's window to prevent deadly sun exposure.

The man turned to leave and in doing so, ran into the unmovable force that was Caliss. The vampire glared down at the human and hissed a snarl. Yelping came from the home's owner as he ran away from the threatening creature.

Caliss brought his icy stare to the transforming young woman curled up on the floor and in a corner. "Feeling any better, my dear?"

"Go to hell," Daniela hoarsely choked out.

She watched the man kneel down in front of her, sneering. "With you by my side." He grabbed her face by the jaw and lifted her upper lip to analyze her forming fangs. "Your rebirth is coming along quite nicely. Not that I'm surprised." He released Daniela's face and continued to loom over her. "You're a very special individual." The backs of his cold fingers sailed over the pale features of the woman's face. The woman jerked her face away from his touch in disgust. "You have made me stronger and for that, I am greatly thankful." He smiled his own, fanged smile and took her hand in his to kiss the top of. "I'm sure you must be hungry." Caliss stood up. "I have prepared you a special meal for your first time feeding." He snapped his fingers and stood aside. Valrae entered the bedroom, obviously displeased and dragging a familiar man behind her.

Daniela recognized this man as the innkeeper from her journey to the monastery. Her eyes looked in horror to the rope bound and gagged man. He was thrown to the floor at Daniela's feet and sobbing for mercy.

Caliss reached down and yanked him to his knees by the hair of his head. Using a talon like fingernail, he cut into the man's neck. It wasn't very deep, but just enough to promote bleeding.

Daniela recoiled further into the room's corner and looked away, squeezing her eyes shut. Valrae scoffed. "Pitiful. A vampire that refuses to feed." She shook her head. "Your second coming is—"

Her words were stopped in her throat by Caliss's hand compressing around it. He growled in warning and tossed the woman back out into the hallway. "Dismiss yourself from my sight as you are no longer needed." With that, the door was slammed in her face to completely rid him of her presence. With a completely changed demeanor, the vampire lord brought his watch back to Daniela. "Never mind her. One's first time feeding is always the hardest."

No matter how hard Daniela tried to resist the monster within her fighting for release, fighting to feed, it was no use. The smell of fresh blood filled her sense of smell and lured her eyes back on the whimpering innkeeper. She unknowingly growled in her unblinking staring of the captive.

There was an animalistic hunger in her eyes. Caliss cutting deeper into the man's neck drew forth more blood. "Feast, my dark angel. Feast to regain your strength."

Completely giving in to the newborn darkness within her, Daniela lunged toward the helpless victim and tore her fangs through his neck.

38

The Siege

"The sisters are coming! They ride close!" A monk could be heard yelling. He rang the monastery's tower bell and repeated his words.

Midmorning prayer was abruptly halted by the present monks looking to each in hope. Abbot Christophe called for them to calm down and remain seated, but the majority of them had already proceeded outside.

Within the dimly confines of the guesthouse, Julian sat on the edge of Daniela's empty bed. His face was buried in his hands and his sheathed swords lying next to him. He could hear the excitement unfolding outside and chose to remain seated where he was.

The house's door bust open, Marcos announcing. "Julian!" He came into view within Daniela's room door, panting. "Have you seriously been sitting there this whole time, since sunrise?" The solemn vampire didn't answer. "Is this all you're going to do is sulk? While Caliss and his followers slaughter towns people and burn everything to the ground?"

Julian got to his feet, growling and baring fangs. "What do you want me to do? Huh? What am I supposed to do when its daylight? Get on a horse and ride off into the horizon?"

Marcos frowned. "You've changed and I'm not meaning your transformation. Used to be you cared about those around you."

Infuriated, the vampire knocked the spear out of Marcos's hand and pinned him against a wall. "You have no idea how I feel about *anything* or *anyone*!" He released the Spaniard and shoved him aside. "If it wasn't for what I have become, I would've gone after David and killed him myself for dare harming Daniela."

A solid form blocked the sun filtering into the guesthouse. William studied his hardly recognizable brother and frowned. "Has the evil responsible for corrupting you finally took hold of your tongue?"

Julian growled and looked to the floor. Marcos was right. He had changed, and it wasn't for the better. He went back into the bedroom to retrieve his swords and flipped up his hood to leave the house. William and Marcos exchanged worried expressions and rushed to follow their troubled brother.

Christophe was speaking with Abbess Frances within the safety of the monastery's interior. They stopped in their conversing to watch the three approaching monks. The abbess took one look at Julian disapprovingly. "I had a feeling you would be trouble." The monk gave a light hiss in retort. "For over twenty years, my sisters within the abbey never faltered in their tasks. No matter the extent of the attacks, that girl was always safe. I let her out of my care for roughly a month and a half and what happens?" She snorted. "Everything the Sect has fought to prevent is ruined. You go get yourself turned and let the girl be taken!" A sterner hiss in warning came from Julian. "Had I not known any better, I'd say you let it happen on purpose! Funny how she gets taken after you're changed!"

It took both Marcos and William doing their best to restrain the monk. Christophe made sure to block his way to the provoking abbess and glowered at her. "That is a bold accusation, my lady. I can assure you, Brother Julian did everything in his power to see to Miss Daniela's safety. The corruption was within the hearts of two men serving these walls . . . not their blood."

Christophe let his own growl be heard and his eyes become blood eyes. Frances backed away from the abbot, eyes wide and jaw hung open. She held a hand to her cross necklace and began reciting passage beneath her breath.

He continued. "Evil comes in many types, Abbess. Not all touched by the damnation feeding on these lands have a corrupted soul."

The woman continued to recite prayer, William looking to his easing brother. "Let us pray Miss Daniela is among them."

*　　*　　*　　*

The darker the skies became, the more boisterous in number the crickets chirping. When night had finally fallen, so did an eerie chill over the monastery. In each tower stood two archers, Jordan among them. Between them were standing stacks of arrows. Any able body capable, helped in preparing a mass supply of arrows. Their linen wrapped tips had been anointed with a paraffin to ignite with fire when the time came.

Patrolling the walls and keeping all eyes to the fields and tree line were more combat ready devotees. Below the perimeter walls and out of any offender's line of sight were lesser experienced combatants wielding spears.

Julian was among those patrolling the wall and staying particularly close to his brother. Though William wasn't fond of fighting, Abbot Christophe felt him someone valuable to help defend.

William looked to the two hatchets in his hands, frowning. "I should be in the infirmary. When the fighting starts, there will be those needing medical attention."

Julian kept his eyes alert beyond the perimeter wall. "When the fighting starts, Brother, you won't have to worry about tending to the injured." He could see William look to him in confusion. "The vampires will be out to kill."

The younger monk gulped and reexamined his make shift weapons. "How do I even use these?"

"Downward thrusts, like cutting a limb from a tree."

William whimpered and kept firm grip on the hatchets. Miles off in the distance, a streak of lightning filled the air. Echoing of thunder wasn't far behind, nor was the smell of raid. "Lovely," William sighed. "And here I was just about to say at least it isn't raining."

"Leave it to you to hex the moment."

William arched a brow at his brother. "This coming from the one who's cursed?"

Julian gave a sideways stare to his brother and cracked a faint smile. The other started laughing and soon, both brothers were laughing.

Frances stood, hands before her and eyes focused on the two monks. Standing next to her was Christophe. "We're on the brink of a possible battle with the vampires with they laugh with no regard to the severity of the situation."

The abbot watched the two brothers and frowned. "Let them enjoy what time they can. There is no telling what awaits us during the night or the day. These moments might be their last, together."

*   *   *   *

Rain fell upon the monastery and all outside its walls. The once choir of crickets in the grass and frogs in the woods gradually came to a stop. All was quiet. A tree falling somewhere within the depths of the forest could he heard.

William spoke. "Sounds like a tree just got uprooted from all the rain. The ground must've gotten too soft." Slow passing minutes later, another tree falling could be heard. The monk arched a brow in intrigue. "The ground must've gotten really soft."

In the passing time, the storm sailed over and the clouds start to dissipate. Lightning from the onward moving storm cell still filled the sky on seldom occasion. In between breaks in the clouds, the position of the phased moon suggested sunrise wasn't too far away.

An unnatural chill set in through the layers of clothing, Christophe opening his eyes from his praying. He breathed, "They're here."

Abbess Frances studied him from the corner of her eye. "How do you know?"

Christophe shot his attention to the bell tower and ordered, "Sound the bell!"

The monk manning the bell tower did as told, everyone both outside and inside the monastery walls coming alive with panic. William searched the darkness of the lands, shrugging. "I don't see anything! There's nothing out there!"

Julian unsheathed his swords, eyes unblinking and staring off ahead of him. "Abbot Christophe is right . . . they're here."

Lightning webbed across the sky, highlighting everything beneath it. Indistinct running at a high speed through the wheat fields widened the physician's eyes. He yelled out as loud as he could, "Brace yourselves, Brothers and Sisters! They attack!"

Weapons were raised and people poised for attack.

The first wave of attackers crashed upon the perimeter wall. Blades impacted the bodies of the intruders as blood spilt onto the stone ground. Limbs were slashed and heads sent rolling. There was no time to properly dispense of the slain. Stopping, if even for a moment, would mean death.

Through the flashes of lightning, idle figures were unmistakable in the vast field. All around them were others knelt down and clawing at the ground. They waited for their master's order to attack and were becoming more impatient. Among them, a figure in a gray dress stood beside Caliss. First glance would mistake them for Valrae, but a second closer look revealed it to be Daniela.

Julian yelled, "Daniela!" His calling out got the attention of several others fighting to see what he saw.

In his being distracted by seeing the ill-fated young woman, a vampire came running up to him. William panicked. "Julian, behind you!"

The monk ducked to avoid an oncoming attack and quickly acted to position the attacker at his back. Around its neck was his right sword's handle to hold it in place. "Archers!" Julian beckoned.

He twisted around to expose the restrained vampire to the nearest tower and a nun took aim with a crossbow. A bolt impacting the target resonated throughout its body. Julian continued to spin around and with his left hand's sword, caught the attacker at the collar bone and cut through to the side.

Seeing the top of the wall become overran, Marcos bounded up the stairs to join Julian and William. The three stood with their backs to the other, slashing their weapons while providing assistance to the other.

On the ground level, Henry had his favored daggers and fending off any vampire getting through the defensive front line. The monastery was being over ran from the north and west walls.

A force slammed into Henry and sent him to the ground. He rolled over onto his back to see a vampire lunge at him. He fought with the creature, trying to keep it at distance while reaching for one of his fallen blades. "Somebody help me!"

Julian heard the cry and finished off his opponent. He knew jumping to his fellow brethren's aid would leave William and Marcos vulnerable. His increased strength and agility was proving to be of great use. The monk had to act quickly and thought of what he could do to help. He hurled one of his swords through the air like a spear.

It struck the vampire in the back and through its chest. Henry saw the tip of the blood soaked sword inches from his face and yelped. The vampire fell to the ground, wailing in pain. Protruding through his back was the sword's hilt. Henry took the sword from the grounded creature and threw it at one of Julian's two attackers. The blade burying itself in the enemy's side ceased its attacking.

Still deflecting his other attacker, Julian reached for his other sword. He took the weapon and slashed across the torso of the second vampire.

From out in the field, Valrae snorted and crossed her arms over her chest. "Tell me, my love, is this how you imagined your glorious defeat over the Sect's most fortified monastery?"

Caliss hissed a growl. "Bring out the catapult. Have those towers and walls brought down."

Valrae laughed sadistically. "It's about time." She glanced over her shoulder and gave a nod to a bald man standing near the tree line by the main road.

The man smiled and began laughing to himself and disappeared into the woods.

Caliss continued. "When the wall falls, Valrae, I want you to lead your contingent into the monastery. Take out that damn monk, first and foremost. After that, kill whoever you want, but save the old man for me."

39

Hope's Falling

Arrow after arrow Jordan shot landed on his target. Some shots weren't exactly where he intended them, but they were affective none the less. It seemed for every one vampire he shot, another three would take its place. How many vampires could possibly be left?

He loaded another bolt and in doing so, glanced out to the field. There was still a group of roughly twenty gathered around Caliss. His attention didn't remain on the vampire lord very long when movement budding through the tree line forced his eyes to it. Being hauled out of the eclipse of the woods' concealment was a rather large wooden structure; a catapult.

Nestled within its bucket was an emblazoned boulder.

He had to warn the others. "Catapult!" Jordan pointed in the direction down the main road. "West wall! West wall! *Incoming*!"

Julian shot his awareness to the tree line just in time to see the fiery boulder be launched into the air. It grazed the side of the front, west tower's midsection and onward into the forwardmost section of the church. The tower, with Jordan inside it, started to crumble from the impact. To the ground it fell and burying its occupants beneath the brick rubble.

Julian looked away from the sight, eyes clenched tightly against the anger and grief swelling within him.

Another fiery bolder was launched off, this one aimed a bit lower than the previous and directly striking the west wall. The structure cracked under the force of the impact and started to crumble.

William chopped through a vampire's shoulder attacking Marcos and panted. "Would really help if those London reinforcements were here." Another hack aimed at the back of the vampire's neck severed the spine.

Marcos impaled a vampire through the heart with his spear and hoisted them over the wall. Waiting for it was an angry mob of armed monks on the ground level.

The Spaniard grunted and rolled the stiffness out of his shoulders. "London's army won't be here for another three days. That's if they travel nonstop."

"We'll be dead by then."

Bricks and rock rained onto the ground upon a boulder impacting the bell tower. Julian looked back out to the field to see Caliss, Daniela and Valrae gone. "Keep an eye out," he announced to the others defending the monastery. "Caliss is on the move!"

Abbot Christophe slashing at the knees of a vampire sent him to the ground. A strong slash severed most of the neck with a final motion completely finishing it off. He tossed the head aside by the hair and glanced around. He had heard what Julian said and knew he was the vampire lord's intended target. For two hundred and fifty years they had chased the other in determination to rid of the other person.

Christophe saw it as a means to finally finish what he started in putting his family to rest. Maybe now, he could finally find inner peace. His hunting gray eyes searched the many faces for its target. All that greeted him were witnessing his beloved monks fall to the ground. Blood spilt from vampires sullied the once sacred ground. It was all making sense to Christophe now. The reason why Caliss allowed so many villagers to be changed was not to overtake the monastery's defenses. With the holiness of the ground corrupted by evil of spilt vampire blood, Caliss's power wouldn't be weakened.

Christophe grew fearful. Caliss was coming after him. He wanted him dead because he was the only real threat, aside from the Sect, stopping the vampire lord from completely consuming England.

The abbot bellowed, "Fall back! Into the sanctuary! Quickly, fall back!" He turned and stopped in his tracks.

Staring back at him and only inches away was Caliss.

"Abbot . . . looking rather exhausted." The vampire lord sneered.

Christophe thrust his sword into the gut of his rival, but it had no influence. Caliss laughed and wrapped his right hand around the other man's. The abbot could feel his sword be slowly withdrawn from its target. He tried to counter the force being asserted against him, but it was of no use.

Caliss was much stronger since being empowered.

He balled up his left hand's fight and slammed it down onto the abbot's right forearm, snapping bone. A swift backhand sent Christophe to the ground and a gash along his right cheek.

Christophe lay there, dazed and trying to come to. He knew he didn't stand a chance going against the must stronger vampire. Nearly all his time was spent on holy ground since being transformed. Holy ground already weakened vampires, even if in brief exposure. To reside on it for close to two hundred and fifty years had worn greatly on him. The church had given him the chance to stay elsewhere and regain his strength, but he couldn't leave those he led by themselves at the monastery. He was a shepherd of his flock and felt obligated to remain there for them.

Caliss knelt down and took the priest by the hair of his head. He reached for the long sword lying on the ground and held its point below the owner's chin.

Caliss laughed. "Had I known it was going to be this easy, I would've done this a long time ago." Before he could thrust the blade upward, he let out a roar in pain. He brought his hand and eyes to the source to see a spearhead protruding through his lower abdomen.

Behind him, Marcos further drove the weapon through the vampire.

Caliss growled and grabbed the plating behind the spear's tip and started pulling out of him. The monk was astounded by this and stumbled backward to put distance between him the creature. Caliss thrust the spear into the monk's left shoulder and roared out in pain, again.

Christophe had gotten back on his feet and stabbed through the top of the attacker's back. The vampire lord tossed the monk aside, ripping the spearhead out of his shoulder. He returned his fighting to Christophe. The butt of the spear was brought around to viciously strike the abbot against the head and into a wall. Clattering of the sword falling on the ground revealed the man no longer being armed.

Julian entered the cloister from the opposite side of the two combatants and went motionless in horror. Caliss impaled the abbot with the spear through the chest. "*No!*"

He tried to push his way through the many people fighting for their lives. He had to try and help save the abbot from an almost certain death. If it wasn't for the overhead sun, he could run through the cloister grounds. Since he couldn't, he resolved to running around it using the shade cover from the arcade.

A sharp blow to the head stopped him and sent him to the blood saturated stone walkway. Valrae sneered over him. "You're not going to stop me, this time."

"He won't have to," came William's voice behind her.

As soon as she turned around, he planted his right hand's axe into her forehead. Using his left hand, he exerted what energy he could muster into cutting through most of her neck. Bringing his axe above his head, he made another downward hack to sever the neck and body. The monk kicked the body into the sunlight for it to burn. Glaring hatefully at Caliss, William held up the head still mounted on his hatchet's blade into the sunlight. Flames erupted from the head as chunks of charred flesh fell to the ground.

Caliss saw this and roared a yell in uncontrollable anger. In retaliation, he buried the spear further into Christophe and gave it a firm twist. Free flowing blood flowed down the black robes and onto the stone flooring beneath them.

Christophe clutched at the wooden shaft of the weapon and felt his feet be lifted off the ground. He was forcefully pushed to the soft earth of the cloister and into the sunlight. The spear was further shoved though his body to pin him in place. His painful screams filled the cloister air and even ceased several people fighting.

The vampires cheered for their master's long awaited defeat of his rival.

Both monks and nuns were appalled by the scene and faltered in their attacks. Their adversaries took advantage of this and struck while the opportunity was available.

Caliss looked to his charred hand and sneered at the blistering skin starting to gradually heal over. His ice cold, bloodshot eyes met Julian's hazel ones and he motioned for the monk to attack him.

Julian shouted out in rage and charged toward the vampire with both swords held before him.

Caliss picked up Christophe's sword and swung out at the other vampire. Julian dropped to his knees and slid under the blade slashing out at him. Using his left sword, he slashed across his rival's upper torso at an angle. He jumped to his feet and deflected a slash from Caliss with his left sword. Using his right sword, he caught the vampire's upper left thigh with another attack.

Flashes of metal cut through the air in hopes of striking the other. They dodged the attacks they could while parrying and deflecting the others. Julian dodged one slash only to get cut across the back of his left leg. He snarled out and dropped to his injured leg's knee. Since on a lower level, he swung his left blade out to cut across Caliss's right knee. He raised his right sword to slash at the vampire's neck, but his hand was grabbed and painfully bent.

His grip on his sword faltered, Caliss getting to his feet. He kicked the monk's left sword out of his hand and bent down to jerk the other man upward. His stronger hand wrapped around the monk's lower face and threw him against a wall, holding him there.

Caliss growled. "The Sect has gotten soft over the years. I was hoping at least *one* person here would be a worthy opponent."

40

The Ultimate Sacrifice

Caliss's grip on Julian's bloody face tightened, causing the monk to let out a moan in torture. The vampire bared his fangs and stated in a growling voice, "You are nothing!" He vehemently heaved the wounded monk to the stone floor of the arcade.

Julian was not about to admit defeat. He might've failed in protecting Daniela and save Christophe, but he was not about to fail himself. As he fought to regain his balance to stand, his attention drifted to a woman in a gray dress. Daniela.

She almost glided in her strides through the chaos of bloodshed across the cloister. Her dress was clean and she seemingly untouched by anyone's attacks. Had she been hiding to avoid conflict or did people know better than to assault her?

Everything inside the monk came to a stop. He couldn't think, let alone move. Seeing what she had become shattered him. Pain tore at his throat and quickly came to realize he was yelling at the top of his voice to her. "*Daniela!*"

Bloodshot green eyes gave a sideways stare in her silent, sinister smiling.

Caliss let out a vicious laugh and brought his attention back to the apparent heartbroken monk. "You see, she belongs to me now. We are one . . . connected by blood." Julian watched the woman continue to walk away, disappearing behind the many combatants. "Join my side and become my second in command. As it stands, the previous holder of such title has been reduced to ash."

Julian's tear glazed, hazel eyes shifted upward to stare into the callous gaze of the vampire lord. "I'd rather die than *ever* serve you."

Beneath the adjacent arcade, William saw his brother stumble to get up, only to fall back down. "Julian, *no!*"

"So be it, then." Caliss brought the tip of his sword to the back of the monk's head and deviously sneered. "Such a pity too. You had great potential to be so much more."

Searing pain shredding through his hand stopped his nearly striking down at the vampire beneath him. Steam was beginning to emanate off his hand and blisters start to form.

Julian recognized this. He had the exact same thing happen when he exposed his hand to help Marcos. How was this happening? They were standing in shadow of the cloister's arcade.

Daniela's crying out captured several people's attention. She was standing just shy of the sun's ray filling the cloister with her hand outstretched from the safety of the shadows. She withdrew her burned and smoking hand from the direct sunlight and began to cradle it against her chest.

The woman shot a vengeful glare at Caliss and spoke. "What was it you said, *love?* We are connected by blood?"

Caliss yelled out in anger as Julian's breath seized in his chest. He yelled out to the woman, meeting his gaze and extending her other hand into the sunlight. "Daniela!"

Her face distorted into pain and another scream erupt from her. Caliss was determined to kill the man at his feet, but it was becoming increasingly difficult. His grip on the sword's hilt weakened and the blade fall to the ground.

He snarled, "Get the girl!"

Daniela saw a supporter of Caliss run toward her. She quickly brought her tear streaked face to Julian and sobbed sympathetically. There was something unmistakably real in those eyes; love. "Kill him, Julian. Kill him—*now!*"

Daniela threw herself into the sunlight and allowed herself to become fully consumed by the brilliant rays. Her attempted captor's hands felt his fingertips brush against the fabric of her dress before out of reach.

Caliss dropped to his knees and shrieked out in agonizing pain. He clawed at his bloodying shirt and ripped it to shreds. Beneath was his searing skin breaking open in several rupturing blisters.

Julian screamed to her, begging her to stop. He tried to get to his feet and save the woman, but a pair of hands held him back. The vampire fought for release, tearing at whoever was stopping him. Had he not been weakened from his injuries, he could've escaped and saved her.

William's grasp was relentless against his brother's clothes. The painful cries of Daniela burning as well as Caliss's from his blood boiling within his veins couldn't mask the torturous heartbreak in the monk's begging to be let go. Fighting between the vampires, monks and nuns came to a halt in their watching the scene.

Caliss clawed the stone floor and coughed up blood.

William watched the gruesome scene as Caliss tried to stand, only to collapse in defeat to his weakening state.

Julian knew now was the time to kill the vampire lord, but he couldn't take his eyes away from Daniela's burning form. She lay huddled on the cloister ground, her strained cries sickening to hear. Even after her sobs were no more, the flesh of her lifeless body still burned.

Julian fell back against his brother, incapacitated by his own heavy sobs.

William shook his brother. "Kill him while he's weak! Now is the time! We must kill Caliss!"

Julian brought his attention to see the bloody vampire knelt over, clutching his chest. Not wasting any more time, the monk gathered his twin swords from the walkway's stone floor. He painfully allowed himself to stand and approached the gruesome form. He growled, "Who's the nothing now?"

Julian held his swords outward and swung them into each other in an attempt to sever the vampire lord's head.

William cried out to his brother in warning, but it was too late.

Caliss had grabbed Christophe's long sword off the stone floor and impaled the younger vampire's chest with it. He twisted and wrenched upward to impose more injury.

William ran to the defense of his brother as Caliss slowly withdrew the sword's blade from the other man. He supported Julian before he could fall to the ground and relentlessly kicked the other vampire in the face. Caliss was sent unconscious to the ground, William embracing his brother.

The monk spoke to the grievously wounded vampire in his arms, hoping to not lose him too. "You're not going to die on me, Brother. You can't die this way, remember? The stories Abbot Christophe would tell us?" Julian coughed for air, clutching to his newly obtained injury and wincing in pain. "You're head has to be severed and your body burned, remember? Surely you do."

Julian hoarsely spoke. "Damn it, William, you're terrible at keeping people motivated to live. Do you treat all your patients with such bedside mannerisms?"

All around them, more cries in pain filled the air. What vampires hadn't fled within the monastery's interior for hiding were being forced into the sunlight to burn. Corralling them were what remained of the monks and nuns from the battle.

Henry ran up to the two, seeing Julian almost covered from head to toe in blood. "Brothers!" William wasn't looking much different. He looked around, mind panicking. "Where's Caliss?"

William looked to the pools of blood where the vampire lord should have been. His cried out in near hysteria. "He got away! We let him get away!"

Julian felt stricken with sickness and brought his attention to the charred form of Daniela in the cloister. "She died for no reason. I let her die in vain."

Henry frowned in sympathy at the two men. What was said was true. They had a perfect opportunity to finally rid the world of the demented son of Lilith, but didn't.

Henry shook his head. "No, she didn't. Remember what Abbot Christophe told us? A vampire can quickly recover from external wounds like cuts and such but it takes much, much longer for one to recover from internal injuries. Daniela used their blood connection and sacrificed herself to make Caliss burn from the inside. That's going to take a very long time to recover from. We don't yet know he got away, in the first place. Its daylight outside! Where is he going to go?" He tossed his hands upward to motion to the sunny skies. "He's got to be somewhere in the monastery. He wouldn't dare try to escape during the day after obtaining the injuries he has."

Julian wiped his face with a blood soaked sleeve, further smearing what was already caking his features. William took one of his brother's arms and wrapped it around his neck. The vampire groaned in protest to being moved, growling. "Find him. Search every rafter and every room. If he is here, I want him found and killed. I'm not exactly in my greatest condition, or I'd hunt the bastard down myself."

Henry continued. "Your wounds are external and can be quickly healed with proper rest and feeding. Caliss, I'm sure, won't rest seeing how he knows he's too weak to take us on. Should he have escaped, he'll keep running, which will only slow down his recuperation. He doesn't have a true family like us to help their wounded."

The vampire felt grateful for the help, yet a part of him felt unworthy of it. "You shouldn't help me."

"And why is that?"

Fresh blood came from the corners of Julian's mouth during a coughing spasm. "Because I'm a monster."

Henry shook his head. "No, you're not. Look at Abbot Christophe. He was a vampire and wasn't a monster."

Julian watched in deep sadness as a nun placed a cloak over the charred form of the woman who sacrificed herself. He spoke. "I will find that bastard Caliss and I will make him pay for what he has done here, today. He will pay for those he slaughtered."

William cut in. "You're not doing this alone."

"It might take an eternity to accomplish, but it will be done. You all are human and too frail to fight an army of vampires. Not to mention, you will inevitably die with time."

Henry replied. "I think we did well today for frail humans. You're the vampire here, and who is it that is too weak to move?" Julian gave the monk a stern stare.

William chimed in. "Besides, who says we're going to be human?" The vampire glanced up to his sly smiling brother.

Henry took the injured monk's other arm to better support him. "Come, let's get him inside so we can tend to his wounds."

Julian didn't like being taken care of. He tried to support himself and cried out in pain. His strength was too weak. He finally gave in and allowed himself to be carried to his old bed within the dormitory. Lying down had never felt better.

William started to remove the bloody robe and called to Henry nearby. "I'm going to need fresh water and clean rags."

The monk nodded and left the dormitory, running down the corridors to the kitchen. Julian winced in pain at the other man's analyzing the many cuts running along his body. The stab wound at his side hurt the most.

Julian studied his brother and shook his head. "I'm not biting you, Will. This is a curse I wish on no one."

William reached for a nearby stack of clean handkerchiefs and pressed one onto the blood oozing stab wound. "Then I guess I'll have to bleed you out myself and drink the blood."

The vampire met his brother's stern hazel eyes in a mixed expression of disbelief and panic. "Like hell you are." William's pressing onto the stab wound a bit harder caused Julian to jerk in pain. He shoved the hand away from assisting him and bared fangs.

41

The Blood of Rebirth

Henry returned to the room with the water and stopped in the doorway. The water bucket was dropped to the floor beside his feet. He felt sickened and brought a hand to his face instinctively. No matter how hard he tried, he was unable to remove his gawking off the scene before him.

Seated on the edge of the bed and wrapped up in Julian's forceful grasp was William. Blood ran down his bare chest as the feasting vampire behind him gripped the monk's jaw, turning his head to allow a better angle for biting. His face and upper body were drawn up in pain, his hands tightly gripping the bedsheets.

Henry reached for his blood-splattered cross around his neck. "Brother Julian, what have you done?"

William opened his mouth to reply, but a choked-out cry came instead. Spikes of paralyzing pain tore at every part of his body and mind. Julian slowly broke away from the bite and took his brother's hand to place it on the free-bleeding wound. Henry nervously grabbed the bucket and cautiously approached the bed.

The monk hastily went to the bedside and wrung out a rag floating in the bucket of steaming water. He removed William's hand and pressed the rag onto the now swelling wound.

Julian collapsed onto the bed and used one of the handkerchiefs to wipe off his face. He stated to his brother, "I have to be careful in the transformation process. Your body could have a negative reaction to the venom and could kill you if introduced too fast." He took in a deep breath of air, continuing, "If it wasn't for Abbot Christophe's assistance, I would've died from it."

Henry allowed the weakened William to lean against him as he tried to keep pressure applied to the still-bleeding bite. "Hopefully it doesn't. Why?" He looked up to the vampire. "Why bite your own brother?"

"Better me than someone else," the man replied. "With me biting him, he'll have retained more of my strength versus someone further down the originating line." Julian groaned in his lying back down. He still felt incredibly weak from his injuries. "When it comes time to fight Caliss, I'd rather have an army I know will have the strength to put up a good fight. As Abbot Christophe told me, quantity over quality. What does it matter if Caliss recruits more for his army? Unless he creates them himself, they'll be much weaker than those I create."

William coughed out a hoarse response. "That's comforting to know."

The vampire continued, trying to ease his brother's worried mind. "My change wasn't exactly the smoothest. The venom was introduced to my body too fast and it put me in a shock. The process takes two to three days for the body to completely transform. In the meantime, welcome to hell."

Henry removed the rag from the man's neck and frowned to see it still freely bleeding. "The bleeding isn't slowing."

Julian moaned against the protest of his body wanting to move as he sat up. "I know how to stop the bleeding, but it's going to hurt like hell."

William sarcastically laughed. "Can't hurt any worse than what I've just been through."

"It's going to have to be cauterized." He reached out a hand. "Give me one of your blades."

Hastily doing so, Henry handed him his cross knife.

Julian extracted the blade and held it above one of the many burning candles William had lit on the nightstand's candelabra. Taking longer than the monk preferred, the blade started to show signs of heating up.

Once the blade was hot enough did Julian remove the knife from the flame and approach William. Henry removed the rag, allowing the other man access to the bite. He then took hold of William's hands and grimaced at the wound being seared closed. The monk cried out in pain behind tightly clenched teeth.

After several seconds, Julian removed the blade to reveal a blackened streak across the swollen bite mark.

Julian snorted a laugh. "Tomorrow, you get to do this again." William moaned in dread. Henry helped him to his own bed and carefully laid him down. Tears filled the distraught vampire's eyes. He could still hear the painful screams of Daniela echo in his mind. "Brother Henry, please see to it Miss Daniela's body gets a proper burial."

The monk nodded in reply. "I planned on it."

*   *   *   *

Days later, Julian's strength had returned enough to allow him to walk around. The first place he went to was the monastery's cemetery. The skies were overcast, which allowed him the ability to comfortably walk out into the open. He looked to the stone cross headstone, reading Daniela's name. Anger resurged within him. He was determined to find the escaped vampire lord and see revenge.

After the monastery grounds were thoroughly searched, Caliss was nowhere to be found. It was discovered a horse was missing from the stables, as were several changes of robes from the wardroom. The conclusion was met of the vampire lord taking the clothes to wrap up in, for protection from the sun, and fleeing on horseback into the woods.

Also during their searching of the grounds, the gravely wounded Abbess Frances was found. In her arms was a nun she was desperate to keep alive. Julian offered them a second chance, which the abbess accepted and the nun declined. She passed away to her wounds come nightfall postsiege.

Marcos, too, recovered. He was barely alive when found from blood loss due to his shoulder's injuries. William fought to keep his friend and fellow brother alive through whatever means he could. The monk was hesitant to accept Julian's offer, but seeing more of the injured die throughout the day changed his mind.

Movement from the corner of Julian's eye shifted him back to reality. He glanced over to see William join him. His skin was clammy versus its once natural, healthy tan from working outside.

Henry joined the two and rolled his shoulders. "This is going to take some getting used to."

William snorted a laugh. "I can get used to it. I feel better than I ever have before."

Julian looked back at the cross tombstone and narrowed his eyes in anger. "I swear, I will get my revenge and kill Caliss. No matter what it takes or how long it takes."

William nodded in agreement. "Till death."

Julian met his brother's gaze and smiled deviously. "Till death."

*   *   *   *

Armored men on horseback, roughly thirty in number, came to a stop outside the monastery grounds. The captain of the riders visually examined the destroyed west wall and crumbled towers. A rider behind him questioned. "It looks like we're too late. Do you think anyone survived?"

Double oak doors opening startled them. The riders expected a flood of vampires to come pouring out and attack them and took arms. A friendly faced nun sporting a cut and bruise on her right cheek came out instead.

She nodded and bowed. "Captain Durik," and motioned into the monastery. "Abbess Frances has been expecting you. They all have, really."

Captain Durik slid off his horse and followed the nun inside. "I must speak with Abbot Christophe."

"My apologies, Captain, but the abbot did not make it." She gave him a regretful frown.

"What of the demon lord, Caliss? His general, Valrae?" He saw the nun wince. "Tell me, Sister, what of their fate?"

"I regret to inform Caliss's escape. As for his general, she was personally dispatched of by Brother William." She stopped to stare the captain in the eye. "I can have her ashes exhumed if you'd like to see for yourself."

There was something in her upbeat voice and the sparkle in her eye that unnerved the captain. "No, no that will be all right. I trust your word, Sister."

The nun bowed and proceeded to guide the knight into the sanctuary. Standing before the altar and speaking with a monk was Abbess Frances. She stopped in her conversing to study the approaching man.

The abbess started walking toward him. "Ah, Captain Durik. I'm glad to see you've finally arrived. We were beginning to think you had been ambushed along your lengthy journey here."

Durik's eyes went to the distinct bite mark on her neck and began to draw his sword. The cold metal of two swords pressing against his throat stopped him. His blue eyes met the stern hazel ones of the monk the abbess had just been speaking with. Julian growled in warning. "I highly advise against that. Should you choose to press on with any kind of attack, I assure you it will not end favorably."

Durik released his sword's hilt, and the blade slid back into its sheath. "What is going on here? Who are you?"

Julian retracted his blades and sheathed them back within the other. Abbess Frances lightly smiled. "Captain Durik, this is Brother Julian. The created son of Caliss and second made grandson of Lilith." The monk hissed a snarl, baring fangs. Frances patted the captain on the hand. "Not to worry, my son. His intentions are pure, I assure you."

Durik and Julian stared at the other, the captain nodding in forced acceptance. "How many of you are there?"

"Just a few," answered Marcos, standing behind the knight and leaning against his spear. He, too, had a bite mark on the left side of his neck.

Durik spun around in sudden fright. He never even heard the second monk come up behind him.

Julian explained as lightly as he could. "To fight evil, one must become it to better battle against it. Caliss is weak and on the run. I see this as a perfect time to build an army to fight against him."

The captain motioned to those around him. "By turning everyone into a vampire?"

"You can either join us, Captain . . ." Julian calmly neared the terrified man. "Or you can get back on your horse and relay message to London of my intentions. Let them try to stop us if they choose." Durik nervously searched the three people's faces, finding nothing but passive stares. "What's it going to be, Captain?"

Durik locked gazes with the obvious creator of the newly formed coven. He could hear his heartbeat pound in his ears and his breathing laboring. Everything seemed to come to a slow around him. Then everything went black.

EPILOGUE

2017 . . .

Lady Ryna hissed from the depths of her containment cell. "She will come from the west, over the ocean and to . . . her . . . homeland."

Her bloodshot eyes stared at the gray-suited Julian. His black leather–gloved right hand rested on a straight cane at his side. His left hand was buried in his pants pocket.

Ryna continued. "Do not worry, my dear Julian *Wright*. You won't have to search far for her. She'll come to you."

Standing next to him were a bishop and two Vatican guards. The vampire growled, "When?"

"Soon." Ryna slithered out of the shadows to look into hazel eyes. "Very soon. I suggest you better hurry though. Seven hundred and thirty years later, he has regained his strength and is on the move."

Julian looked to the bishop. "I need to get back to my hotel in London . . ." He strode past the religious figurehead and two guards. "To warn my people to be on the lookout."

The bishop stayed at the man's heels. "What about you?"

"I'll do what I always do."

Ryna didn't restrain her laugher, its maniacal tone echoing in the dungeons.

*   *   *   *

Onboard a 747 and asleep in their middle-aisle seat was a young brunette in her midtwenties. Her head tossed about in fretful dreaming. Suddenly, she snapped awake, green eyes wide in fright. Seated at her right was a young black woman close to the same age. To her left was a young white woman, and next to her, a teenage girl bearing a strong resemblance.

The young black woman studied the other passenger in concern. "Danny? Are you all right?" No answer came. "Danielle!"

The young woman Danielle jerked her head to the right. Green eyes met dark brown. "Huh? Yeah, yeah I'm fine, Mica." She huffed a deep breath and sunk into her seat. Her heart was frantically beating in her chest, and she wondered if anyone noticed. "I just had a bad dream, is all."

"You sure," came the left-side passenger's questioning.

"Yes, Stephanie, I'm fine, okay?" Danielle leaned her head back and closed her eyes, trying to calm down. "Just . . . ready to get off this damn plane, is all. I can't feel my ass."

The teen sitting at the far left of the center-aisle seat cut in. "What do you expect from a seven-and-a-half-hour flight from New York to London?"

Danielle didn't answer and lightly grabbed her neck. Her nightmare felt so real. So familiar. Those icy blue eyes set in a haunting face. Where had she seen the man in her dream?

Mica patted her hand excitedly and pointed the view outside a window. "There it is! There's London!"

The four friends watched the landscape become larger in the plane's circling around for a landing. As excited as she had been for this London trip since last year, a part of her felt coming here was a big mistake.

Hopefully she was wrong.

SUMMARY

In thirteenth-century Europe, a war between good and evil rages. A rare blood offering unique qualities to any vampire that bites them is born after two hundred and fifty years. As a secret division within the church, known as the Sect, struggles to keep them protected, a villainous vampire lord will stop at nothing to get the blood for himself. He is determined to fulfill his fate set down by his demonic creator, Lilith. Will the church prevail in their goal of protection, or will all hope be lost to the clutches of evil?

Printed in Great Britain
by Amazon

21771285R10111